Revolutions of All Colors

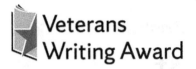 **Veterans Writing Award**

Sponsored by the
Institute for Veterans and Military Families
and Syracuse University Press

In keeping with Syracuse University's longstanding commitment to serving the interests of veterans and their families, Syracuse University Press, in cooperation with the Institute for Veterans and Military Families (IVMF), established the Veterans Writing Award. We invite unpublished, full-length novels or short story collections in manuscript form for consideration. This contest is open to US veterans and active duty personnel in any branch of the US military and their immediate family members. This includes spouses, domestic partners, and children. We encourage women veteran writers and veterans of color to submit. Although work submitted for the contest need not be about direct military experience, we seek original voices and fresh perspectives that will expand and challenge readers' understanding of the lives of veterans and their families.

Revolutions of All Colors

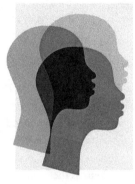

A Novel

Dewaine Farria

Syracuse University Press

First Edition 2020
20 21 22 23 24 25   6 5 4 3 2 1

∞ The paper used in this publication meets the minimum requirements of the
American National Standard for Information Sciences—Permanence of Paper
for Printed Library Materials, ANSI Z39.48-1992.

For a listing of books published and distributed by Syracuse University Press,
visit https://press.syr.edu.

ISBN: 978-0-8156-1126-4 (hardcover)   978-0-8156-5515-2 (e-book)

Library of Congress Cataloging-in-Publication Data
Names: Farria, Dewaine, author.
Title: Revolutions of all colors : a novel / Dewaine Farria.
Description: First edition. | Syracuse, New York : Syracuse University Press,
    2020. | Summary: ""Revolutions of All Colors" is a novel that follows
    the lives of three black Americans as they confront the uniquely American
    dilemma of cobbling together an identity in a country still struggling to
    define itself. Farria stitches together myriad points of view and overlapping
    time-frames to tell a story of evolving masculinity and friendship in the midst
    of racial and sexual politics, fatherhood, and war"— Provided by publisher.
Identifiers: LCCN 2020025267 (print) | LCCN 2020025268 (ebook) |
    ISBN 9780815611264 (hardback ; alk. paper) | ISBN 9780815655152
    (ebook)
Subjects: LCSH: African Americans—Fiction. | Blacks—Race identity—
    Fiction. | United States—Social conditions—Fiction.
Classification: LCC PS3606.A7378 R48 2020 (print) | LCC PS3606.A7378
    (ebook) | DDC 813/.6—dc23
LC record available at https://lccn.loc.gov/2020025267
LC ebook record available at https://lccn.loc.gov/2020025268

Manufactured in the United States of America

For my father,
Command Chief Master Sergeant Karl Lewis Farria,
USAF (ret).

America's history, her aspirations, her peculiar triumphs, her even more peculiar defeats, and her position in the world . . . are all so profoundly and stubbornly unique that the very word "America" remains a new, almost completely undefined and extremely controversial proper noun. No one in the world seems to know exactly what it describes, not even we motley millions who call ourselves Americans.

—James Baldwin, "The Discovery of What It Means to Be an American," 1959

Contents

Revolutions of All Colors

1 | Desire

New Orleans, Louisiana
June 1970

ETTIE COULD NO LONGER ignore the woman with the tambourine. Not now, with the pianist thudding the mahogany lid over the keys, and the heavyset boy who'd lathered over the drums for the last hour clutching his sticks perfectly still in the storefront church's compressed humidity. Cocooned in sticky silence, the musicians blinked perspiration from their lashes, eyes locked on the woman with the tambourine. All of True Vine Baptist Church—from Ettie, so fiercely expressionless that her face might have been carved from ebony, to the teenagers who'd spent the service flirting and dozing in the back, to the old folks in the first three rows waving cardboard hand fans advertising Moore's Funeral Home—all focused on that tiny copper-colored woman, draped in sunlight from the open windows behind the pulpit.

The woman raised both hands, shuddering the tambourine against the air, and finally rapped it against her palm. Then she started to sing.

There's a lily, in the valley. Briiiiiiight as the morning star.

Oscillating fans shunted a muggy breeze around Ettie's ears, as the choir followed the woman's lead.

Ohhhhhhh, there's a lily, in the valley, briiiiiight as the morning star.

The words seeped, a cappella and raw, merging with the hum ascending from the congregation. Punctuated by the Amen corner's pitch-perfect clamor of *hallelujah*s, *yes Lord*s, and *well now*s, a primordial pull—at once warm and grave—throbbed so powerfully through True Vine that, for a moment, Ettie's mask of indifference slipped. She surrendered to the lilt of the hymn, nodding into blissful belonging alongside the other sweat-glistened faces, and it felt like home.

From the pulpit, Pastor Putnam removed his glasses and mopped a silk red handkerchief across his hazelnut brow. Putnam looked in the direction of Ettie's father, Roland, who tensed like a hunting dog at her side.

"Deacon Moten, join me at the pulpit for the altar call."

Roland squeezed Ettie's knee. Then, alabaster vial almost hidden in his coal-black mitt, her father strode to the front of the church, towering next to Putnam at the pulpit.

Ettie hadn't been to church in the three years since her mother's death. Enough time to have kind of forgotten about altar call. Before Wynnie's death, this used to be the part of the service when—as she sat sandwiched between her parents—Roland would whisper "Lilli-Putnam" in Ettie's ear. Wynnie would lean forward in the pew, not looking directly at either of them, but blinking slowly and ensuring that both husband and daughter saw the pinched expression under her church crown. Roland's oft-repeated Swift reference never failed to set father and daughter trembling against each other with suppressed laughter.

From the congregation, Ettie studied her father now—hands clasped around the pale vial, chin to his chest, eyes squeezed shut. The same expression Roland wore at Wynnie's funeral. Not distraught or heartbroken, but searching—struggling with all his might to figure out what came next.

After the funeral, he and Ettie had sat on their porch in the Tremé, watching a burst of steamy rain pelt the sidewalk. Ettie placed her arm around her father and he collapsed onto his only child's shoulder. Ettie laid her head against her dad's, breathed in his worn-leather scent, and knew she wouldn't be leaving for Spelman that fall.

Ettie enrolled in the predominantly white Tulane University, and Roland—through his connections in the city government—found her a part-time position at the Housing Authority of New Orleans.

In the meantime, deaconing morphed from a nod of community respectability for Roland into something more like a lifestyle. Sunday morning services and Bible study on Wednesdays. Then Sunday evening service and choir rehearsals on Tuesdays. And finally, Thursday night Steering Committee meetings, topped with weeklong church revivals that sapped her father's time and energy in a way that left Ettie wondering if it wouldn't be easier to just go to hell. Since her mother's death, Ettie wasn't sure which of her parents she missed more.

The woman struck the tambourine again, this time on her hip, and her voice swayed through the humidity like ink in water.

Somebody's found peace, in the valley. Briiiiiiiight as the morning star.

With the sound of a great sizzling, half a dozen tambourines from the choir and congregation joined the chorus all at once. *Amen. Aaaaaaamen. Aaaaaaaaaaaaamen-hmmmmmmm.*

Ettie closed her eyes and saw shadows huddled outside slave quarters at dusk, belting out these same prayers. All those years. All those prayers. The thought that her people—her own father—needed this celebration of capitulation to get through their days grounded Ettie in the moment. Here, among True Vine's long-suffering Negros, and their conviction, despite all evidence and experience, that the best response to oppression was more love, more forgiveness.

Since Wynnie's death, Ettie treated her day-to-day at HANO—every plumbing and trash removal complaint—as if it were all that stood between her people and the tide sweeping them into a state of permanent underclass. With the exception of her dark skin and wiry, almost outlandishly corded figure, Ettie had inherited very little from her mother. Certainly not her faith. One should question a faith that so readily betrayed its believers.

Nothing was destiny and no one, celestial or otherwise, was coming to save them. The only sentimentality Ettie allowed herself was the occasional daydreamed rewriting of history according to what *ought* to have happened. Fantasies she'd never admit out loud: tiptoeing into the plantation big house, palms clasped over thin lips, blades pressed to pink throats—imagining those who had driven her ancestors gurgling crimson snot bubbles while gasping their last into dark unsmiling faces.

At the pulpit, Roland looked up from his clasped hands, directly at Ettie, and boomed out a "Yes, Lord!" that staccatoed through her spine.

"I know that many of you came here this morning burdened beyond words," Putnam said. "But the Lord wants you to know, you don't have to carry those burdens alone." He swept the sleeve of his clerical robe toward the congregation. "The altar is open."

Ohhhhh, there's deliverance, in the valley. Briiiight as the morning sun.

"Lord, you are the stars! And the wind between the stars! You are the feather in the flame!" Putnam's bouncy evangelical cadence plucked some chord in the congregation that no longer pulsed in Ettie. All the worshippers on her pew shot to their feet, arms outstretched.

The pastor raised his palms. "My hands ain't clean! But I've stood still in the rain. I've weathered the storm!"

The lady on Ettie's right waved lace-gloved hands as if directing a plane onto a runway. "Praise your name, Jesus!"

Ettie inched her bony backside in the opposite direction along the wooden pew, catching the intense—almost hungry—stare of a dark-skinned young man with an ex-con's telltale thick neck and forearms. The sort that church mothers recruited with a couple home-baked pecan pies during prison outreach. The young man mouthed something in Ettie's direction. It took several moments for Ettie's face to reset to her default *Negro, please* expression.

A teenage boy stepped into the aisle behind them. Evangelical murmurs of approval cascaded through the congregation.

"Oh, glory hallelujah."

"Bless his name."

"We worship you, Jesus!"

Ettie recognized the boy, Ernest, a standout basketball player in his senior year at her alma mater, Carrollton, New Orleans's most prestigious colored school. At church potlucks, Ernest never failed to finagle a story out of Roland about his stint playing ball at Grambling or as an officer in the freshly integrated army. Roland, who'd since worked his way up to a managerial position in the city's department of public works, always indulged the youngsters, and himself, with a tale or two of his glory days. There were a lot of things about her father that Ettie wouldn't have known had it not been for Ernest.

The teenager bounced to the pulpit, Afro bobbing with his ballplayer's gait.

With a hand raised to the choir, Putnam softened the hymn to a ghostly chant.

> *Ohhhhh, there's peeeeeace in the valley, briiiiight as the morning sun.*

Ernest whispered into Putnam's ear, growing increasingly animated, miming his plea. The pastor's eyebrows arched.

Ettie's eyes narrowed as her father passed the alabaster vial to Putnam. The pastor dabbed a finger in the container, before handing it back to Roland. Even from the height of the pulpit, Putnam had to stretch to his tiptoes to trace an oil cross on Ernest's forehead.

"Lord," Putnam raised his voice. "Ernest here comes to you the only way he knows how—humble, meek, and mild—with a plea only you can address."

> *Peace in the valley, briiiiiiight as the morning sun.*

"Lord, you said you would never leave us, nor forsake us!" The minister burst into a lyrical spate of tongues and pressed his palm onto the teenager's forehead. *"Shohanah nah nah sohee."*

"We praise your name, Jesus!" Roland's words reverberated off the church walls like the beats of an oak drum.

Ernest's hands rose from his sides.

Putnam jittered like a shaman possessed. *"Nononana hana shee!"*

Roland stepped down from the pulpit behind Ernest, preparing to guide the young man to the slatted wooden floor.

When she was ten years old, Ettie asked Wynnie what it felt like to be slain in the spirit.

"Like unconsciousness." Wynnie got a faraway look in her eyes. "Like blissful unconsciousness."

Ettie preferred to be present.

Despite Putnam's glossolalia conniption fit, Ernest did not collapse.

Eventually, Roland placed his hand on the teenager's shoulder and led him back down the aisle to the congregation. As Roland passed, he shared a faint smile with his daughter. Three years after Wynnie's funeral and he'd finally gotten her back to church, even if only for that one Sunday morning. But for Ettie, seeing Ernest keep his feet in True Vine still felt like some kind of victory, like some cause for hope.

✤

After that, Ettie couldn't stop bumping into Ernest, always in the Ninth Ward and usually in Desire. As a Housing Authority of New Orleans client service representative, Ettie covered all the downtown housing projects: Desire, St. Bernard, Florida, Lafitte, and Iberville. Isolated from the rest of the city at the end of the Bywater bus line and cloaked in rotten-egg stench from the Agriculture Street landfill and the Industrial

Canal, the Desire Residential Development was by far the worst neighborhood in the city—more open-air prison than housing project.

The first couple times Ettie spotted Ernest, running hard with the local boys on the courts across from Paulin Street, she had been rushing—clipboard in hand, blouse sweat-plastered to her chest—from beneficiary meetings to utility-service checks, navigating the sea of ebony, copper, mahogany, and beige faces surging to and from the sprawling development's single bus stop.

Late one evening, after following up on a complaint of "rats big enough to saddle," Ettie paused near a crowd watching a group of glistening, shirtless young men in a four on four. She wasn't a sports fan but had been roped into watching enough games with her former college-jock father to know that all these boys could ball. But when Ernest gave the guy guarding him a check and a couple feints at the top of the key, Ettie understood everything she needed to know about this matchup. Ernest had these boys shook.

Ernest blew through the lane as if his defender's Chuck Taylors had melted onto the court. Then instead of kissing the easy layup off the backboard, Ernest dumped the ball off to another member of his squad, who took an off-balance jumper at the top of the key.

The ball whizzed through the chainless rim, and Ernest was back on defense before it hit the asphalt.

"Nice shot, KJ. Back on D now." Ernest's voice was level, calm. "A'ight, man up. Man up."

On the sidelines, residents cautiously attempted to draw Ettie into conversation on everything from the weather ("humidity thick enough to spoon-feed a baby today") to the forgiveness of the rims ("those gotta be the Ninth Ward's kindest backboards"). Ettie tucked her clipboard into her damp armpit, nodded, and made the sound of laughter when appropriate.

Wynnie's pretensions to New Orleans's colored aristocracy had left a yawning psychological gulf between Ettie and the communities she served. A class division manifested in an excess of "white"-derived manners and interests that commitment to her job alone could not bridge but that didn't seem to affect the likes of Ernest or Roland in the least. Athleticism's capacity to render men—from janitors to stockbrokers—mutually palatable annoyed Ettie to no end.

Ernest spotted Ettie and lifted his chin in her direction—an imperial chin lift—without taking eyes off his opponent. He picked a guy's pocket at the three-point line, snatching the basketball with an authority that seemed to settle some unspoken argument. Then he rifled the ball to a teammate near the sideline, whose hands had to have smarted from the projectile's force.

Ettie was reminded of a film of the Soviet dancer Mikhail Baryshnikov she'd seen during a course on Eastern European culture: the feeling of watching a very specific type of human doing exactly what he'd been engineered for. The game should have been a blowout, but since Ernest never took a shot—every time he had a clear lane to the rim, he dumped off to a teammate—the matchup remained close enough to leave the small crowd cheering.

In the game's decisive turnover, Ernest planted his high-tops and took a charge so flagrant that even the culprit didn't try to deny it. Ernest had been feeding this goofy big-headed KJ kid all game, and finally set him up for the winning layup. Even

Ettie couldn't help but laugh at KJ's "That's what I'm talking about!" cry of victory that heralded the end of the game.

Neighborhood kids swarmed Ernest and a few of the other young men after the game, savoring the last few moments of the late July evening, before the streetlights came on and their mothers started calling.

Ettie watched Ernest push away from the chain-link fence on the edge of the court to greet the dark-skinned man who'd tried to speak to her at church.

"Hey, Ettie!" Ernest called. "Come on over here for a minute. I want you to meet somebody." Ernest gestured to his companion. "This is Troy. He's with the Panthers, just got in from Oakland."

Ettie felt her shoulders drop.

Her cautious optimism at the first rumors of a New Orleans branch of the Black Panther Party for Self-Defense had given way after seeing a few of the out-of-towners passing out flyers and whatnot on campus. Thugs with Afros and clenched fists, sprinkling the fairy dust of left-wing platitudes on their pimp fantasies. "If we can't sit at the table let's knock the fucking legs off it." And not all the quips that fell out of those boys' mouths were all that left wing. "Shiiiiit, the only position in the Black Panther Party for women is supine." And her favorite, directed at the fawning antiwar white girls: "How about you gimme some of my civil rights tonight, baby?"

West Coast transplants elbowing their way into the country's oldest urban black community without so much as a nod to folks like Ettie—already on the ground, putting in the work. Her HANO routine might not have been flashy—no berets or sunglasses—but it was the most effective way she'd found of actually improving people's lives.

"Hey. I saw you in church a couple weeks ago." Troy smiled, extended his hand. "Too good to talk to anybody."

"Nope," Ettie said, giving his hand a firm, quick shake. "Just too good to talk to you."

Troy laughed, surprising her.

"That lady sure could beat that tambourine," Troy said.

"What?"

"That's what I was trying to tell you in church." Troy didn't stop grinning.

"Yeah, well, you must have missed the part when they flip those tambourines over into collection plates," Ettie said.

Troy guffawed.

"Come on now, Ettie," Ernest said. "Pastor Putnam and them help people get by. We need that."

"Yeah. The struggle to get by grinds people down every day. But that damn sure don't ennoble the acceptance of oppression." Troy spoke deliberately, as if this was his first time expressing this idea with these particular words. Or maybe he was just politicking for the small audience of youngsters listening in on their conversation. "Don't forget: slaves were expected to sing while they worked."

Ernest waved off Troy.

Ettie and Troy exchanged glances. Ettie looked away first.

"Besides." Ernest shook a finger in Ettie's direction. "You know your daddy wouldn't be up in there so much if True Vine was all bad." He turned back to Troy. "This lady's father was a captain in the field artillery. Won the Silver Star."

"Where'd he serve?" Troy asked.

"Korea." Ettie paused. "You served?"

Troy nodded.

"Where?"

"Folsom."

Ernest laughed, nudged Ettie, then, noticing her expression, straightened up.

"Right," Ettie said. "Well this was a real pleasure . . . Troy? It was Troy, right?"

"We started our free breakfast program for working families last week." Troy tilted his head, ducking his dark, regal face—like some Ethiopian prince, except with a nose shaped more from pugilism than genetics—into Ettie's line of sight. "You should check it out."

"I'm surprised you have time for it," Ettie said, preparing to insert some deliciously deviant grammar into her speech. "What with all them white girls I see y'all chasing on campus."

"You've never seen me on campus," Troy said.

He had a point there. She would have remembered.

"Look. No one's saying the Panthers descended from revolutionary heaven. But these are good, solid brothers. And I did hear that the Desire HANO rep, Miss Et-tie Mo-ten"—he enunciated the four syllables of her name with just enough pomposity to get her attention—"gives a shit. So, pretty please with sugar on top, stop by and see what we're doing. It might be we could do some good together."

Ettie *mmm-hmm*ed and was on her way.

"We're across from the Broussard grocery," Troy yelled at her back. "On Piety Street, just outside Desire."

"Smooth," she heard Ernest say. "Real smooth, Troy."

But now only Ernest was laughing.

❀

When Ettie spotted Troy outside the Broussard grocery a few days later, he immediately broke into that grin. Whoever heard of a smiley militant? Troy held up a finger to the folks he was talking to and, stepping through a swarm of gnats dancing above an overflowing storm drain, walked toward her.

The Panthers' Piety Street Headquarters was just outside Desire and, like the rest of the housing project, seemed on the verge of a fetid mud slide into the Industrial Canal. The smell of excrement in front of the Broussard grocery that morning was so strong that Ettie's eyes had begun to water.

"Miss Ettie Moten! I guess you do give a shit."

Troy's too-loud greeting further grated Ettie's nerves. She hesitated before shaking his hand. "I guess that's high praise."

Behind Troy, children raced ahead of their parents into a building pockmarked with plywood windows and the Black Power posters that Ettie knew all too well: Huey Newton's iconic throne shot, the viciously misogynistic Cleaver looking uncharacteristically pensive, and a rare one of Fred Hampton with the butt of a rifle resting on his hip.

Squinting in the muggy funk, Ettie didn't see any familiar faces among the families on the street. Still, she recognized these folks: women with chemically bruised hair peeking out of head wraps, dressed in the thick grays and plaids of janitorial staff; men in work boots and Dickies or vigilantly maintained threadbare suits; ashy-kneed children who sometimes didn't get enough to eat because the bills always ate first. Proud people living in circumstances that did not encourage self-respect. The sort of folks Ettie only spoke to from across a desk or while carrying a clipboard.

Ettie felt that familiar barrier rising as the families' stares transformed her—with her melting mascara, flats, and sensible maroon blouse—into the Establishment. A seething mass encompassing everything from landlords, to bosses downtown, to the police. Despite her dedication to the job, Ettie knew that for many of these people she was worse than the man—a silver-spoon coon whose relative privilege was even tougher to swallow.

Arms akimbo and T-shirt stretched across his shoulders and back like a drum, Troy nodded toward the Panthers' building.

"We make sure all these kids get a good meal before their shift," Troy said, referring to the "platooning" of Desire's overstuffed elementary schools.

"A half day of school is not enough," Ettie conceded. Then her eyes narrowed, as she watched Troy absentmindedly nod to a young father and son. "But I work in the world as it is, not as I'd like it to be."

Troy nodded again, this time in her direction, and displayed his palms in mock surrender. "Fifty percent education, but a hundred percent taxes. The least we can do is make sure they don't spend their time in class hungry." Then he brightened. "At least they're getting you for their money, right?"

Troy led her to the shade on the cracked sidewalk.

"We have a little neighborhood cleanup thing going on Mondays, Wednesdays, and Fridays," he continued. "On Tuesdays and Thursdays, I teach a political education class. We had the first sickle-cell anemia screening a couple weeks ago." Troy stopped short, looked at her. "You ever know somebody with sickle-cell?"

"No."

"My cousin used to keep us up nights screaming from that pain," Troy said. "Just affects black folks, so ain't nobody researching it."

"How many of y'all are here?" Ettie asked. "Panthers, I mean."

"Fourteen brothers." Troy looked at Ettie again and seemed to decide something. "Double the number of Panthers the police have killed during the four years of the party's existence."

"I see you, Broussard!" Another Panther—whom it took Ettie a moment to peg as a black-bereted Ernest—yelled at a heavy-jowled white man in crimson suspenders hurrying into the grocery behind Troy.

"You better not raise them prices next week." Troy's sweet face grew cold as an executioner's, and he shouted with vein-bulging intensity, "You hear me, motherfucker!"

Ettie took a step away from Troy.

Broussard slunk into the grocery.

Ernest and Troy slid their hands across each other's forearms, clasped fingers, and brought their palms together with a crisp, martial clap. After a moment's pause they nudged elbows and bumped knuckles, finishing with fingers fluttering to the sky.

Ettie noticed a group of kids watching with stares on full beam. Kids already indoctrinated in the Deep South's concentration camp culture. Kids whose parents walked on the same side of the street as white folks only when absolutely necessary. Kids who'd witnessed their parents scraping in front of men like Broussard their entire lives. Little brown boys who'd slipped out of the house before their mommas could get Vaseline on their elbows and knees. Little brown girls with beaded braids the color of the rainbow. Kids whose world's boundary just barely reached the edge of government offices downtown.

The importance of that tiny moment of insurrection in these—their—children's lives struck Ettie hard. More than simply replacing the services of an absentee state and corroborating the injustice in this community's daily existence, the Panthers legitimized a feral sort of black masculinity. Yes, many were misogynistic, arrogant, and dangerously naïve. But they were also young, black, and unafraid. And Ettie suddenly understood just how important it was that their kids saw *that*.

A few feet away from a rancid, overflowing storm drain, Troy and Ernest agreed that Broussard was a punk motherfucker. That settled, they turned their attention back to Ettie.

But before they could speak, Ettie had already asked, "How can I help?"

✿

Over the next few weeks, Ettie helped Troy expand the breakfast program to include day-old bread and fresh fruit from some of the left-leaning grocers downtown. She didn't join the BPP outright (Troy was adamant on this point), but her presence, and tacit endorsement, lent authority to the New Orleans cohort. In turn, the Panthers provided Ettie the cultural heft that she'd been longing for. Ettie stopped wondering if the community she served loved her back.

During the phone calls that, over the course of the summer, became their evening ritual, Ettie and Troy crafted the speeches he gave in front of rooms containing sizable chunks of all the left-wing political money in the American South. Troy commented that the best parts of these speeches came from Ettie, and—while they both knew that wasn't entirely true—she reminded him not to forget it. Ettie's position precluded her from publicly spouting fire-and-brimstone speeches like Troy, but she didn't try too hard to dissuade rumors of her complicity in devising them.

"I won't trust those white lefties until one of them loads my gun," Troy quipped over the phone. They'd just finished up work on a speech he would deliver to some "aboveboard sponsors" the next day.

"Write that one down," Ettie replied, cradling the phone between her shoulder and cheek, cord stretched onto her porch. "It'll be a good line in your autobiography."

"Yeah, right." Troy laughed.

This was the closest Ettie allowed herself to flirting with Troy, and he never pushed it. Given Ettie's initial impression of the Panthers, Troy seemed determined that she take them—him—seriously.

Their talks sometimes lasted until "The Star-Spangled Banner" had signed off every TV station and Ettie, for the umpteenth time, had assured Troy that, yes, she was well aware of the anthem's racist theme. Despite the buzzing barracks lifestyle he shared with "the brothers," Ettie suspected these chats were the only time Troy could truly let down his guard.

"Why don't you come with me to meet those sponsors tomorrow?" Troy asked.

"Yeah?" Ettie glanced back at the hook-latched screen door to see whether Roland was within earshot. Her father had a knack for finding things to do wherever she happened to be on the phone.

"Absolutely. It'll shake them bleeding hearts up to see me flanked by someone else besides baaaaaad-ass Panthers." Troy sighed into the phone. "Besides, I want you to see what it's like dealing with folks comfortable with us as victims, but not as men."

The following day, July 20, 1970—the hottest day on record that year—Ettie found herself at a Students for a Democratic Society meeting in a moss-covered shotgun house just outside the University of New Orleans, annoyed. A thin layer of perspiration coated her face and dark patches expanded at her armpits. But when Troy began speaking, Ettie stopped dabbing her handkerchief on her forehead and sat up.

At an oak podium with a microphone stand shoved to one side, Troy performed calisthenics with words. He was so unlike the Panthers Ettie had heard on campus who lobbed scripted, flat-from-overuse catchphrases back and forth like ping-pong volleys.

Power to the people.

Absolute power to the people.

When the people have power, then we can make this earth civil and humane.

Every day the people are out of power is another day of the madness.

Not Troy. He spoke in simple truths that struck like thunderbolts.

"Civil rights? To hell with civil rights. Proper sanitation, access to healthcare and education, equal protection under the law. These aren't exceptional things. These aren't civil rights. They're human rights."

"Our struggle ain't unique. Look at the Brown Berets, the Vietnamese, the Palestinians. Shiiiit, look at Stonewall. This is bigger than just us. This is global revolution. Everyone participates, whether they know it or not."

"You Troy Shaw?" activists from out of town would ask. "They told me I need to catch one of your classes while I'm down south."

In front of a crowd, pride hovered around Troy like an unfailing light; Ettie had never met someone who occupied that space so well.

But when Troy talked about the police, the rational coalition builder vanished, and his rhetoric slipped into combat fatigues. Justice would be the main course, but with a side of vengeance.

"Nah. Nah. I won't lock my doors because of the pigs. I just make sure my guns are loaded and leave those motherfuckers open. Shoot straight, I say. And aim for the nose."

The white liberals in the room applauded with the enthusiasm of Stalin's Politburo. "It's not me," their desperate nods and utterances of "right on!" seemed to plead. "*I* get it."

"We ain't going to hum spirituals while barbarians unleash dogs," Troy seethed. "We ain't going to pray for the establishment to produce reasonable human beings. They murdered compromise with King. You can't compromise with the monster. You *have* to kill it."

Later that day, over celebratory po'boys at Dooky Chase's in the Tremé, Troy commented, "It's funny, back in Oakland the sight of white people was something ominous, like storm clouds gathering."

"Is this the part where you tell me Shaw is just the name one of your ancestors received on an auction block?" Ettie asked.

"Well. Yeah. Wait, hold up a minute." Troy gave her a frightened look. "Did I already tell you that?"

Ettie laughed. She had to admit, he could keep up.

"Seriously though: the most dangerous creature in the history of the world is a white man in a suit. Before I joined the party, I knew three, maybe four, white people by name. Now I can't get away from them motherfuckers." Troy blew a raspberry, looked around the restaurant, then smiled. "This place is a good start though."

"Damn straight," Ettie said.

The Tremé was her neighborhood, and Ettie had touted Dooky Chase to Troy as one of the best—and blackest—restaurants in the city. From Billie Holiday to Sammy Davis Jr., Dooky Chase's eggshell walls boasted photographs of virtually all the country's black elite, and it had been her mother's favorite restaurant. Ettie's unmitigated love for Dooky Chase's po'boys trumped her reflexive aversion to any place so adored by the colored aristocracy.

At the sight of a hunk of oyster-laden French bread balanced between Ettie's long, delicate fingers, Troy—sounding uncannily like her father—teased, "The queen and her oyster po'boy."

Ettie winked and licked her fingers. "And she's loving every bit of it."

Troy heard quite a lot about Roland from Ettie, but not vice versa. Ettie planned to tell her father about Troy once there was something to actually tell. And she certainly didn't tell Troy everything about her dad. Like Thurgood Marshall, whose portrait they sat under now, Roland was a firm proponent of the war in Vietnam.

Ettie had finished half her sandwich when Pastor Putnam entered the restaurant.

From Putnam's generic greetings, Ettie could tell that he didn't know any of the patrons. But the pastor didn't let that stop him from speaking to everyone.

"How you doing, brother?"

"Hey. How y'all doing?"

The diners nodded. "All right, Reverend."

Ettie watched Putnam politicking his way toward their table and realized that success as a revolutionary or a reverend both hinged on community acceptance.

"Sister Ettie!" Putnam spoke as if he wanted to include the entire restaurant in their conversation. "You spoiled us, showing up for service at the beginning of the summer like that. How you been?" Then, without waiting for an answer, he asked, "Who's your friend?"

"I'm fine, Daryl," Ettie replied, enjoying how Putnam's face marbled in indignation at being addressed by his first name. "This is Troy."

Troy pushed his chair away from the table, brushed his palms down his thighs, and stood.

The two men shook hands.

"I've seen you at service," Putnam said.

"Yep," Troy replied. "I was recruiting."

Folks in the restaurant shifted in their seats at the sight of the pint-sized pastor, in his crisp white-collared dress shirt, grasping the hand of the prison-buff Black Panther in shirt-sleeves. Ettie wished that someone would take a snapshot to add to Dooky Chase's collection.

In a voice that reminded Ettie just how much of the world's unhappiness is perpetuated by small men, Putnam broke the silence. "Tell your father I said hello, young lady."

The pastor continued to a room in the back marked "Private Parties."

Troy sat down. "Your family's close to that guy?"

"My mother was. And my father . . ." Ettie paused. "You know what? Even while my dad was clowning the church, he never stopped trusting in it."

"Clowning the church," Troy repeated, his relentless grin shrinking to a guileless half smile. "You better not let Roland hear you talking like that."

Ettie found herself popping into the Piety Street headquarters a couple evenings a week. Troy's favor made the younger Panthers almost comically respectful to her. Over the course of the rest of the summer, she found herself taking a couple puffs of the joints the Panthers passed around while play-fighting over the eight-track, cleaning weapons, and talking shit of the purest male bravado variety. The cohort oscillated between treating Ettie like a mafia matriarch and forgetting—with startling regularity—that she was present at all.

"Ahhhhh, man!" Ernest, the baby in the room, piped up through air thick with the smell of weed and cordite. "I know this motherfucker ain't putting on Edwin Starr again!"

They elevated "five on the black-hand side" dap handshakes to high art and discussed the subtleties of Afro Sheen with an interest altogether contrary to their affected machismo. Ernest would treat everyone to sticky, sweet Sno Balls from the stand on Paulin Street, and one of the older Panthers—one of the veterans or ex-cons—would unfailingly flick the high schooler in the testicles during the walk back to the office. Swift, vicious backhand strikes so perfectly timed that even Ettie couldn't help but chuckle.

"Goddamn it, Clarence!" Ernest would howl, doubled over and trying to balance his cup of flavored ice.

Troy referred to Clarence—a gold-toothed, cornrowed bruiser with the face of a sad clown—and the other Vietnam vets as "former candidates for death through conscription." Soldiers of a different stripe than Ettie's father. Brothers who'd watched their officers through narrowed eyes, fingers tapping their rifles' trigger guards. Others were ex-cons and hustlers who'd squared up and now discussed revolution with the same ease they'd once talked about serving junkies through peep-holes. No NAACP choirboys or stuffy Nation of Islam dev-otees, the Panthers were headbangers and proud of it. All so young that guys like Troy and Clarence, in their midtwenties, seemed ancient.

Stoned on the couch in the Panther office, Clarence would mouth-trumpet into his fist and announce, "Her Majesty, Queen Ettie the First."

Ettie would curtsy on the shag carpet and smile into Clar-ence's eyes—a pair of bloodshot orbs, already long gone from this planet.

Clarence stayed high. He'd show up, toss a bag of weed on the coffee table, and wink at the youngsters.

When Ernest tried to call Clarence out by asking why he spent so much time talking to white girls on campus, the Viet-nam veteran responded that he was with them only for the giggles.

"Giggles?" Ernest asked.

"You know." Clarence licked his teeth. "If you listen real hard while a white girl's blowing you, you can hear our slave ancestors giggling."

Then there was sandbagged headquarters itself, with the neat rows of Molotov cocktails stacked under the chicken-wired windows. And the guns. So many guns. Afros bowed around a table of overflowing ashtrays, a highly contested chessboard, and plastic cups half full of white port wine and lemon juice, the Panthers doted on their arsenal. Ettie cringed at how even Troy joined the cohort in polishing and stroking those guns with an affection worthy of the large-breasted Afrocen-tric women who shared space with Che and Malcolm on the walls. They had everything from high-powered 30-30s and sawed-off shotguns, to big pistols like the .44 and .357, all the way down to derringers that they concealed in their socks. Cheeks nestled against rifles and marijuana smoke curling from their nostrils, the Panthers let the satisfying crescendo of *clak-clak*s convince them of their invincibility against the pigs.

"Freedom," Troy was fond of saying, "has a nice ring to it. And some recoil."

☸

Mr. Beaucamp, Ettie's supervisor at HANO, called her at home early on the morning of September 16, a Wednesday.

"All regular government services to Desire are suspended until further notice. I want you in the office today."

"Why?" Ettie asked, intentionally not specifying which statement she was questioning.

Mr. Beaucamp audibly sucked at his teeth over the phone line. "Read the paper."

Ettie replaced the phone in its cradle on the kitchen wall. Beaucamp was the kind of white man that Troy wouldn't have known what to do with. The kind who made sure Ettie got all "Outstandings" on her evaluations, but could write a dissertation on why General Lee deserved a traffic circle in his honor in the center of the city.

"Work?" Roland asked over her shoulder.

"Yeah. Your buddy Mr. Beaucamp."

"Oh, he loves you." Roland chuckled, poured himself a cup of coffee. "Do you still have your office in the filing room over there?"

"You know it," Ettie said, remembering how the sides of Mr. Beaucamp's crewcut had crimsoned on the day he'd finally conceded to her transforming the filing room into an office.

"Fine." Mr. Beaucamp glowered over the top of his glasses, his expression one of pure exhaustion. "Fine."

It had been Ettie's first triumph at HANO.

In the kitchen, Ettie pressed her lips to the stubble on her father's cheek, gave him a smile. "I'm running late. Mind if I take the paper to work with me?"

Roland shook his head. "I'll pick one up at the stand." He tipped some milk into his mug. "Go easy on Beaucamp, Ettie. That man's a lot of things, but . . ."

"Lazy ain't one of them," Ettie finished for him.

"All right." Roland laughed. "Watch it, girl."

Outside, bugs, birds, and early-morning commuters were all, as Roland liked to put it, "drowning in the humidity."

Ettie stooped next to the wicker chairs on the porch and picked the *Times-Picayune* up off the concrete porch, which she and Roland had painted a soft tangerine orange the previous summer. Then she straightened, smoothed her slacks with her free hand, and glanced at half the front page. She stopped, blinked, unfolded the paper. A shootout in Desire had crowded Tropical Storm Felice off the front page.

She refolded the newspaper, tucked it under her arm, and—after a quick glance through the screen door back toward the kitchen—stepped off the porch.

Ettie rushed to the corner of the street just in time for the bus up to Touro Street. She slid into a seat near the front and pressed in the metal tabs to wrestle down the window. The bus got going. Ettie drew calm from the breeze before shaking open the paper.

She flew through the article.

The New Orleans morning wobbled past the bus like scenes in an old movie, seemingly unaware of the day's significance.

Catacombed shotgun houses surrounded by weeping willows, the bus driver touching his cap while pulling the door crank with his free hand at each stop.

Finally, the bus lurched to a halt on Touro Street, and Ettie beelined to the row of pay phones outside the HANO building.

Between the newspaper, that frantic first call to the Piety Street Panther headquarters from the pay phone, and her own understanding of the neighborhood, Ettie pieced together most of yesterday evening's events before setting foot in the office.

Two boys who sold the *Louisiana Weekly* on the corner of Tulane and Broad, the location of the Orleans Parish Jail, had outed Clarence and another Panther—one of the other Vietnam vets—as undercover NOPD officers. It was a Tuesday evening, so there would have been a large number of Desire residents present at the Panther headquarters for Troy's political education class. All the low-level Panthers Ettie spoke to on the phone that morning (no one was able to locate Troy) agreed that it had been Ernest who'd thrown the first punch and screamed to let the Desire residents administer "people's justice" on Clarence.

Through a storm cloud of rocks, bottles, and fists, Clarence made a mad dash out of the Piety Street headquarters. NOPD snipers that no one knew were present opened fire from the roof of the Broussard grocery, killing nineteen-year-old Kenneth James Borden.

"KJ." One of the young Panthers told Ettie over the phone, frustration creeping into his voice. "You know KJ. Ernest's boy from the courts across from Paulin Street. Yeah. *That* KJ."

As the *Times-Picayune* put it, "One resident of the Desire Development was killed by covering fire police provided for an undercover officer fleeing the scene."

The paper didn't mention how KJ's corpse lay face down in a puddle of blood for two and a half hours while snipers remained in overhead watch and uniformed police waited for an armored vehicle to buttress their courage enough to enter the neighborhood on foot. Meanwhile, KJ—a light-skinned boy with a big head, gray eyes, and an easy smile—drained into the gutter like roadkill. It was almost ten o'clock when three teenage Desire residents—a girl and two boys—half dragged, half carried the corpse to the police lined up outside the projects.

Ettie hung up the pay phone, leaned her forehead against the glass in the booth, and pictured the looks those black children exchanged with the officers in that moment of absolute clarity, when everyone present understood the precise difference between being a citizen of a state and a ward of it. These, Ettie thought, are the stories communities do not forget. Memories, reminders, lessons that filter like bad blood through a people's collective consciousness. The sort of anger that becomes a family heirloom.

Nervous about using her office line to call the Panthers' HQ, Ettie ducked back and forth from the pay phone outside HANO all day. The Panthers Ettie spoke to said they hadn't seen Troy or Ernest since last night, and she believed them.

Near the end of the workday, Ettie returned from a last attempt on the pay phone only to find Mr. Beaucamp sandwiched between Clarence and a high-yellow, obviously plain-clothes law enforcement officer in her tiny filing room office.

Before Ettie could speak, Mr. Beaucamp held up a palm, then twisted his wrist toward the American flag–lapelled officer at his side. "Ettie, this is Special Agent Sawyer." Beaucamp swept his hand toward a bruised and battered Clarence, who was tugging at the knot of his tie with a bandaged hand. "I think you already know Officer Howard. They have some questions about your caseload."

Then, with relief etched on his face, Mr. Beaucamp left the three of them staring at each other in the stuffy room.

The sun set late in Louisiana's Indian summers, but the filing room's single window, close enough to the neighboring Public Works building to touch, permitted only enough natural light to expose the stagnant dust in the mold-tinged air.

Ettie drew a breath. This wasn't her first dance. She'd dealt with law enforcement at HANO before. Despite NOPD's reputation, Ettie always tried to be helpful and professional with the police she dealt with in the office. Mostly, they asked routine occupancy questions: who was staying where, when.

Ignoring Clarence, Ettie didn't mask her head-to-toe scrutiny of Sawyer. From his hairline that ventured several degrees northward without attaining outright baldness, down to his spit-shined Stacy Adams, and then, scornfully, back up again. No way was this beanpole chump—so light skinned that Ettie wondered if one of his parents was white—going to run the okeydoke on her.

"Hi, Ettie," Sawyer finally said, scanning the room from behind wire-rimmed glasses. "You meet a lot of Panthers here?" His Bostonian brogue whittled Panthers into *Panthas.*

"Here?" Ettie gestured around her workspace. "No. In the Ninth Ward, around Desire, yes. I know the Panthers there." The federal officer didn't react to Ettie's smile while hissing the *s* after her overly crisp *r: Panthersss.* "That's where I met Clarence. On Piety Street. That is your name, right? Clarence?"

Clarence snorted.

Ettie gestured to the heap of manila folders on her desk. "Mind if I file while we do this?"

"Not at all," Sawyer said.

Ettie felt Sawyer watching her fingers shuffle through the labels of the downtown projects. Then Sawyer abruptly ducked under the filing room's single unprotected light bulb and scooted his narrow behind onto her desk.

Sawyer made a show of picking up the framed picture on Ettie's desk. The federal officer looked up from the photograph: Roland in shirtsleeves, thick arm draped around his daughter's narrow shoulders like a comrade-in-arms in danger of falling into a sudden headlock.

Sawyer flipped the picture in Ettie's direction. "Captain Roland Moten, 999th Armored Field Artillery, Silver Star for heroic achievement during the Battle for Imjin River, Korea."

"Put that down," Ettie said, feeling her voice waver.

Sawyer obeyed, looked at her.

"Last night the New Orleans chapter of the Black Panther Party for Self-Defense outed two undercover NOPD officers in its ranks." Sawyer nodded toward Clarence. "Officer Howard walked out. Officer Israel Fields didn't."

"Yeah. I heard about that." Ettie straightened the photograph on her desk without giving Clarence so much as a glance. "What do you want from me?"

Sawyer reached into the inside pocket of his suit coat, withdrew a photograph and placed it on the desk. In the picture, Troy stood in a throng of young men poised in leather-jacketed, black-bereted defiance. Troy gazed straight at the camera with impatience, like some East African prince, the only person in the picture not posing.

"Troy Shaw." Sawyer tapped his finger on Troy's face. "You know him. Where is he?"

"I wish I knew," Ettie said.

"You wish you knew?" Clarence shouted, "You out there running the streets with them boys, cutting a fool, and you wish you knew?"

"Yeah, Clarence," Ettie replied. "I wish I knew, so I could tell him that there's more undercover pigs in his chapter."

Clarence's nostrils flared. "You think I stopped being black after earning this badge?"

Ettie didn't miss a beat. "How's that line working for you on the street, Clarence?" With her fingers, she made quotation marks around his name. "Convince many folks out there that fancy cops like y'all ain't really pigs?"

Sawyer raised a hand, as if quieting quarrelling children. Then he placed another picture on the desk. "This is Officer Fields at the hospital."

Ettie had never spoken to Israel much at Piety Street, but she recognized him in the photo. The cop was lying on his right side on a gurney in a white-walled emergency room, mouth agape. A dark ring of blood haloed his swollen face on the sheet. It looked like Israel should have died two or three times before he reached the hospital, and the NOPD photographer squeezed every bit of it into one excruciating black-and-white shot.

"Where's Troy?" Sawyer repeated.

Ettie paused.

"You want to serve your community?" Sawyer looked Ettie in the eyes. "This is the way to do it."

"I. Don't. Know."

"He'll makes corpses out of those boys," Sawyer said.

"He'll make men of them," Ettie shot back. "And some will be heroes. Some already are. What would *you* have them be?"

"Alive."

"I don't know where Troy is. I've been calling all day. No one's seen him."

"Okay." Sawyer tapped the edge of the two photographs on the desk before tucking them back into his suit coat. "Stay out of Desire tomorrow."

"Why?" Ettie asked.

"That's all I'll say," Sawyer replied. "And I'm saying it for your father, not for you."

Ettie opened her mouth, then closed it. Weighing her words down to the ounce, she turned to Clarence. "Tell them not to move until at least ten o'clock. You know that if they go early that building will be full of kids."

Under his cornrows, Clarence's face bricked in cold rage.

"You're going on the raid, aren't you?"

Clarence didn't answer.

"Of course you are." Ettie gave Clarence a withering smile and held his gaze like a dare. "Clarence?"

"What is it, Ettie?"

"Don't be the first through the door."

On her porch that evening, Ettie repeatedly dialed the first six digits of the Piety Street HQ and then hung up. How much would she tell Troy? After the conversation in her office, Ettie had begun to wonder if it all hadn't been a red herring to divine how much she'd tell the Panthers. Perhaps she shouldn't tell Troy anything at all?

She'd spoken to Sawyer for only five minutes, but he'd struck her as sincere. A jerk, but sincere. A safe, vetted Negro, probably from Hoover's first batch of black agents. Ettie imagined what Sawyer must have endured in *that* institution.

It was too easy to call men with that type of endurance Uncle Toms. Men who crumpled Viet Cong propaganda flyers in their fists (*Black Man, this isn't your war*), took off their helmets, wiped their brows, and continued to march; men who, like her father and uncles, chuckled about the time a white platoon sergeant in Korea called someone a "big-lipped nigger"; men who, in response to dogs, fire hoses, and the charred bodies of little girls in their Sunday dresses, clocked in early. Citizens. Peculiar black patriots. True believers in the American dream despite the yoke. Men who took racism on the chin for the next generation's sake and never budged. "Ignore. Outwork. Outperform." Ettie sensed Roland's ethos in Sawyer.

By the time Ettie finally dialed the seventh number, the sun had finally set, her butt had gone sore on the concrete porch, and she still hadn't decided what to say to Troy.

Someone picked up on the first ring.

"Hello?" Ettie asked, when no one on the other end greeted her.

"Hey, Ettie." It was Troy. "How you holding up?"

Ettie thought for a moment, then answered honestly, "I'm shaken."

"It'd be weird if you weren't. KJ was a nice kid."

"He was."

"Damn shame."

They were quiet for a few moments.

"Let's talk next steps in the community," Troy said.

"What? Now?" Ettie began. "But what about the—"

"No," Troy cut her off. "You and I don't talk about that part of it."

"We don't talk about that part of it?" Ettie repeated, incredulous.

"That's right. We kept you aboveboard for a reason. We need you where you are. And that means we don't talk about that part of it, okay?" Troy let that sink in, then continued. "Listen, I spoke to the brothers about your idea for an apartment sitting service."

"Yeah?" She'd forgotten about that. Ettie's idea was small in scope but, like the breakfast program, the type of thing that went far in building grassroots support in the community.

"Yeah. It's on!" He hesitated, embarrassed at the excitement his voice betrayed about getting back to work. "Come by tomorrow and we'll talk to some of the residents about it. And it'll give us the chance to catch up."

More than her love for him—and it was in that instant that she truly, finally understood that she loved him—the importance of Troy maintaining a continuous heartbeat for the next twenty-four hours suddenly took on a stark clarity in Ettie's mind.

It might have been too late for the Panthers, boys barely out of their teens pursued with the full force, ingenuity, and resources of the US government. Too late for Desire, bursting at the seams with hatred and misery, love and forgiveness. But maybe not too late for Troy. They'd lost too many leaders young.

"Let's start at Alvar Street," Ettie said. Alvar Street was on the opposite end of the projects from the Panther building. "Around nine o'clock?"

In the morning, Ettie made sure that by nine forty-five they were only speaking to the residents in the second of four buildings on Alvar. In the shade of a weeping willow in front of a building seemingly held together with little more than peeling paint the color of rust, Ettie and Troy spoke to two moms and their children.

"Absolutely," Ettie told a young mother balancing a blinking, cocoa-faced toddler on her hip. "The Panthers can assign two men to the building during the day."

The news of the apartment-sitting service—the promise of residential security in a community where police inspired more fear than criminals—enthused the residents as much as it had Troy the eve before.

Ettie fetched back her gaze when Troy tried to meet her eyes, like a piece of jewelry she'd only wanted to show him quickly. Something had shifted between them.

Ettie planned to take Troy to lunch at Dooky Chase's after they finished up here; anything to keep him out of the Piety Street HQ.

An erratic burst of gunfire followed by a sustained salvo jerked their heads away from the families. The torrent echoed between Desire's dilapidated buildings and swallowed Ettie whole, licking the sweat on her back into frost. The first exchange settled into the squawk of bullhorns, which the Panthers cut short with a fresh deluge. Each crack rattled Ettie's bones. Then a pair of thunderous bangs, followed by pylons of thick, angry smoke rising from the direction of the Panthers' building.

Ettie's stomach cinched when Troy drew a pearl-handled Derringer from the small of his back. Troy held the pistol low and cocked his head in the direction of the firefight. Ettie, body trembling like a clenched fist at the incessant barrage, seized Troy's forearm.

"No!" she yelled. "Don't go!"

Not such an odd thing to say, given the circumstances. But something gave Troy pause. Maybe it was her hands' steadfast refusal to remain still. Maybe she held his stare too long or looked away too soon. Maybe until then Troy had been denying something he'd suspected since the moment they met.

Troy gave Ettie that half smile, the one he reserved just for her. His left hand found her waist in what Ettie at first took as an act of kindness but then understood as a sign of the judgment, like some violent shadow passing across the sun.

Troy's pistol arced from his hip and landed squarely on her nose. Hard and level, carrying his full weight, a blow that would have dropped someone twice her size. But force alone didn't cause her to crumble the way she did. Something folded in Ettie when Troy struck her. She fell to the pavement discovered, defeated, and discarded. On the sidewalk, Ettie clutched her face and found that her nose had lost its rigidity. She held her hands there, as if to keep her features from spilling onto the cracked asphalt, looking up just in time to see Troy racing toward the gunfire, pistol at the low ready.

2 | Citizens

I ain't sure which I heard first: the gunfire or folks yelling, "Get down!"

Under the city's new SWAT protocols the cops didn't identify themselves at Piety Street that day, say anything about a warrant, or even tell anybody they was under arrest. They just started shooting.

What'd I do? I'll tell you what I did. I threw myself on that floor, that's what the fuck I did. Shiiiiiit. Them bullets was snapping back and forth just a couple inches above my head, like some goddamned pinball machine of death on tilt. Shotgun slugs pounding the walls like motherfucking sledgehammers. Boom! Boom! Setting us to coughing from all that pulverized brick and concrete.

After that first salvo, we all just laid there quiet for a second, hugging floorboards, waiting for somebody to take charge. Troy wasn't there. Clarence neither, and he was a snitch anyway. It's still hard for me to wrap my head around Clarence not just being a snitch, but an actual pig who gave the FBI chapter and verse on all of us.

Then they started with the bullhorns.

"Occupants of Number Twenty-Seven Piety Street, this is the New Orleans Police Department speaking. Come out with your hands up. Comply immediately and you will not be harmed."

Somebody slid a shotgun across the floor to me. I grabbed it and low-crawled to one of the street-facing windows on the first floor. I looked over and there was that boy Ernest, inchworming to the opposite end of the same window.

Ernest turned his head away from me, mushing half of his Afro against the floorboards. Then he hawked up an oyster-sized wad of phlegm onto the floor. He turned back around, face glistening like a slave, lips crisscrossed with sticky lines of spit.

"Ain't this a bitch."

I couldn't help but laugh.

Around HQ, we was always messing with Ernest. But I'll tell you what, that boy had some vinegar in him that day.

"You ready?" Ernest asked.

I nodded and we both took a quick groundhog peek above the sandbags stacked under the window. And there they were. Row after row after motherfucking row of Cub Scout–uniformed pigs. And every single one of them on those first two rows was black. Brothers back from the war. Just like me.

How'd I react to that? Huh. Well. Try to imagine just how much hate was radiating both ways on Piety Street that day. As a Panther, I loathed all police—local, state, and federal—but none more than the black ones. Just like the pigs hated all of us left-wing radicals—from the Weather Underground to the Brown Berets—but none more than the black ones.

There were thirteen of us in HQ that day, and—no shit—there must have been damn near a hundred officers out there, a good two dozen of them black. They had the street bracketed up with them shiny new armored personnel carriers.

Again with the bullhorn. "Occupants of Number Twenty-Seven Piety Street . . ." They must have repeated that spiel eighteen or twenty times before that morning was through.

Ernest spoke up, pointed at a couple brothers. "Y'all get ready to push that refrigerator up front and bring down some extra ammo."

He held up a fist to halt movement.

"Damn," I thought. "Somebody's been paying attention in armed defense class."

"Hold up," Ernest said. "Wait 'til we open fire to move."

"All right, Ernest," I said, loud and clear, making sure all the brothers understood I was backing the young buck.

"Y'all ready to open up? Y'all ready to open up?" Ernest was nodding like a maniac. "All right, goddamn it! Fire!"

I popped to my knees and let the metal holla on them fucking pigs. Boom! Pump. *Boom!* Pump. *Boom!* Pump. *Boom! Shiiit, got to the point I couldn't tell where the shotgun ended and my hands began. My teeth was rattling from all the muzzles blasting up in there.*

How the fuck did that make me feel?

My dick was hard as a diamond while we was laying down that lead. How about that? Yeah. That's what it was like. Getting off. Hell, I ain't even sure it's worth trying to describe. Either you understand the pure pleasure of getting some or you don't. And if you don't, there ain't no point in me tryna tell you what it's like.

After something like that you can make up whatever bullshit you want—you hated it, loved it, whatever—doesn't matter. It is what it is. But for me, in that moment, I felt absolutely free. We were free Negros. In that little space we had. We were kings. And that's what I felt.

Wayne Kirkland
Black Panther Party for Self-Defense—New Orleans Chapter
Former specialist, Twenty-Fifth Infantry Division, Quang Ngai Province, Vietnam
From *An Oral History of the Black Panther Party in New Orleans*, curated by Gabriel Mathis, March 2007

New Orleans, Louisiana
September 1996

YOU NEVER can tell who's going to get fat.

From the rear of the church, Ettie watched Ernest clench the edges of True Vine's same two-tone mahogany pulpit, drop his chin to his chest, and hum along with the choir.

Wicker baskets had replaced the overturned tambourines as collection plates and the machine hum of window-mounted air conditioners had joined the drone of fans, but otherwise little had changed in True Vine since Ettie's last visit. That is, besides the man at the pulpit.

The twenty-six years since Ettie last saw Ernest had packed a good forty pounds on him, withering his once lustrous Afro into a sad, gray frizzle of its former glory. But Ernest had gotten this preacher bit down pat. Every detail—from that cardboard-stiff collar, to his Crescent City–inflected baritone, to the seamless colloquy between him, the choir, and the congregation—flawless.

Facing Ernest just below the pulpit with his back to the congregation, the conductor—a jet-black man in an electric blue suit—swayed counter to the choir, but in perfect time with it.

The choir conductor pointed to the left quadrant of the even dozen white-and-crimson-robed singers.

"Tenors, come on."

We just can't give up, oh no! We shall receive a reward!

The conductor half sang, half commanded the tenors to "say it again."

We just can't give up, oh no! We shall receive a reward!

"Altos, come on."

Let us not be weeeeary. We shall receive a reward!

The conductor pointed at the center of the choir. "Say it again, altos."

Let us not be weeeeary. We shall receive a reward!

"Sopranos, help me!"

Stand fast! Don't faint! We shall receive a reward!
Stand fast! Don't faint! We shall receive a reward!

Tambourines raced, filling the church like an invocation to fire. The conductor swirled his hands with enough ferocity to fend off a swarm of bees, the seams of his formfitting suit jacket straining over his narrow back and shoulders. "Everybody!"

We just can't give up, oh no! We shall receive a reward!
Let us not be weeeeary. We shall receive a reward!
Stand fast! Don't faint! We shall receive a reward!

The cacophony of lyrics resonated throughout the church, blending into a single, stark melody.

We just can't give up, oh no! We shall receive a reward!
Let us not be weeeeary. We shall receive a reward!
Stand fast! Don't faint! We shall receive a reward!

"Just because you carried it in," Ernest thundered from the pulpit, pausing to adjust a hairline screech of feedback on his microphone, "doesn't mean you have to carry it out!"

The first altar call Ettie had heard since Roland dragged her to church at the beginning of the summer back in 1970.

"Are you still blind to him?" Ernest asked the congregation. "Because he sees you. Oh, yes! He *sees* you. You are a stranger to yourself and yet he knows you."

After service, in an overcast afternoon heavy with that scent of encroaching rain, Ettie hung back on True Vine's creaking covered porch, giving Ernest room to glad-hand parishioners with variations of those old evangelical verbal tics.

"Praise the Lord, sisters."

"Bless his name."

"Today the Lord truly blessed."

Ettie took a breath and stepped into Ernest's line of sight. She'd never let Ernest intimidate her before and wasn't about to let him start now, even with the added bulk.

The preacher's eyes full-mooned.

"Ettie?"

"Ernest. Looking good, old man."

The two stood in front of the crowd of parishioners, sizing each other up. Despite the middle-aged spread straining against his clerical robes and the frizzled non-Afro, Ernest's presence held a vaguely imposing air. After all these years, he'd finally become the big man. Ettie felt oddly embarrassed for *not* having gained any weight in the last two and a half decades, as if her perpetually petite figure and seemingly poreless ebony skin were evidence of some deep-set vanity. She caught him appraising her nose, as if confirming that it was still off-center.

"Dooky Chase in an hour?" Ettie asked. "Let me treat you to a po'boy?"

"So," Ernest said with a wink. "Since I don't have much hair left to cut, you're going to tempt me with oyster po'boys?"

Ettie waited for the parishioners' chuckles to subside. "That sounds like something Clarence would have said."

Ernest's face bricked over with pomposity and what Ettie was almost certain was a glint of malice. He was going to make her pay for that.

"See you there?" Ettie pressed, fanning herself with a church program. "I want to talk about Troy."

"Okay. See you there in an hour."

Then Ernest turned to shake another hand.

🌀

She'd finished half her Oyster po'boy by the time Ernest showed up.

He weaved businesslike between the paisley-linened tables, stopping short to greet a family of seven seated at a table for eight.

"Mother Hanes! Chester still over at Xavier?"

Whoever Chester was, Ernest knew his major (business administration), girlfriend's name (Cheyenne), and every bit how proud his grandmother was of him.

Ernest's stride stiffened as he approached Ettie's table.

"Still in your getup," Ettie said. If he wanted an argument, she was going to give it to him upfront.

Ernest settled into the seat across from her. "This isn't a 'getup,' Ettie." He spoke as if each of his words would be entered into the congressional ledger. "I really am a reverend. This is really what I do."

"Of course. I heard how much you've . . ." Ettie hesitated, but all she came up with was, "changed. Actually, that's part of the reason I'm down here."

"But mostly you're back for the funeral."

"Mostly."

"I suppose it was you who wrote that obituary, then."

"Who else? Why?"

"No. Nothing. It was nice." Ernest leaned back in his chair, folded his left leg over his right thigh. He was about to say something cruel. "I guess if people were really half as good as their obituaries, the world would be a great place."

Here we go, Ettie thought. "Troy was every bit as good as that obituary. And, nah. The world's not a great place. Crack and Jesus keep people around here from noticing it too much though."

Ernest held a hand up to the approaching waiter without breaking away from Ettie's gaze. "I'm going to need a couple more minutes."

The waiter, a skinny light-skinned boy in a pair of tan slacks about two sizes too large, glanced at the menu in his hand before returning to the kitchen.

"The last time I saw you was at the Edward Hebert Federal Building," Ernest said. "The day after the raid. Talking to an agent."

"I know. I saw you there too."

Ernest drummed his argyle-socked ankle and then extended a palm in her direction. "Care to expound?"

"Two uniformed officers picked me up from the hospital the next day and escorted me to the Hebert building. My dad was with me."

"Was he? I didn't see Roland there." Ernest swung his leg off his thigh and for a moment seemed to be speaking more to himself than to her. "But then I only caught a glimpse of you while they was shuffling us between rooms for questioning. I'm sorry I couldn't make it back for Roland's funeral. When did he pass again?"

"'77. October 23rd," Ettie said. Ernest's shift in tone had left her disarmed. "A Sunday."

Ernest wagged a finger in her direction. "Yeah. I remember now. I was on ship. My last deployment before I got out."

"He always liked you." Ettie smiled, looked Ernest in the eyes. "Anyway. Even with Roland, I felt surrounded by all those cops. Gasping through my mouth just to breathe."

"Troy shouldn't have hit you like that."

"What do you know about it?" Ettie shot back.

"Nothing."

"Exactly. You don't know a damn thing about it. Don't pretend otherwise."

"I do know that I was in HQ during that raid, Ettie. Where were y'all? Huh? Where were *you?*" Ernest snorted, brushed the back of his hand against his mouth, then gestured toward Ettie's face. "I'd almost forgot about that," he said, and only then did she feel the sneer on her lips. "That's one thing Clarence was right about: that superior contempt of yours. For everybody. No one reached Queen Ettie's standard."

He paused, took a breath. "But, yeah. You're right. All I know about your nose is that it was just one bad thing in the middle of a lotta bad stuff that went down that day."

Plainclothes officers securing the perimeter of the operation identified, tackled, and arrested Troy before he reached the Panthers' HQ. After an hour-long gunfight the thirteen young men on Piety Street surrendered anyway. The officers led the Panthers—carrying their seven wounded comrades—to the waiting NOPD vans.

In response to a reporter's question about the ethnicity of the officers who spearheaded the raid, New Orleans Police Chief Joe Giarrusso responded, "They were Americans. Citizens."

The Panthers were all eventually acquitted for their actions in Desire. The Panthers' guns were legal. The FBI's counterintelligence program—COINTELPRO—was not.

"I'm sorry, Reverend," the waiter's voice seemed several octaves too deep for his uncreased face. "But do you want a menu?"

"Son." Ernest tapped his fingers on the tablecloth twice. "I could recite that menu to you blindfolded."

The boy laughed, deferring until the older man was ready to proceed.

"I'll take the shrimp Clemenceau and an iced tea," Ernest said. "Sorry about the wait."

Ettie wished she had ordered that. Then, watching the boy push through the swinging doors back to the kitchen, it occurred to her that Ernest *was* a reverend. This *was* what he did.

"I let them raid that building full of my friends, Ernest. And I didn't say a word. Not one word. To any of y'all. Only tried to save Troy." She gestured to her nose. "Maybe I deserved this."

Ettie continued quickly. She didn't want to hear Ernest's response to that.

"Giarrusso and them said I might be asked to testify later. Said I didn't have to change my name, but I did need to leave New Orleans."

"Where'd you go?" Ernest asked. "Your dad wasn't saying, and nobody else seemed to know."

"Oklahoma. Counseling at one of the prisons up there." Ettie sat back in her chair, worked a crick out of her neck. "Actually, I'm head of correctional counseling services for the whole state now."

"Of course." Ernest grinned at her.

At Antoine State Prison in Oklahoma, Ettie saw the worst of her race but also some of their best. Some of their proudest, bravest, most daring, most enterprising, most undefeated. And she advocated for every two-bit hustler as if he were a political prisoner.

"You want me to do Troy's service?" Ernest asked.

"Yes." She paused. "And I want you to talk to his." Another pause. "My." Finally she smiled. "Troy and my—our—son."

✿

The decision whether to see Troy—when Ettie found out he was serving time on an unrelated bank robbery charge back in California—was not really a decision at all.

It was 1977. The first week of December. A little over a month after Ettie had buried her father.

Their son, Simon, was born in '79.

Ettie fidgeted in the visiting room during that first visit to Folsom.

But then there was Troy with that grin.

"Well, Ms. Et-tie Mo-ten." He flattened his palm on the glass, his posture that of someone completely comfortable in the room. "I guess you really do give a shit."

3 | Walking Point

Antoine, Oklahoma
September 1996

HOPPED UP on a cocktail of quaaludes and speed, Sergeant Willie Kearns stormed into the mess hall and murdered three white soldiers. Then Kearns slumped to his knees, braced the butt plate of his rifle on the floor, and pressed the warm muzzle into the flesh under his chin.

That's how I always pictured it, anyway—foam leaking out the sides of Kearns's mouth, sizzling on the flash suppressor—so that's what I told the boys.

It was a bright, apple-crisp Sunday morning. The garage door was at half mast, and a few autumn leaves had gathered on my gym mats.

I dug my hands into my kangaroo pocket and took a breath, turning from Simon's hungry stare to my own sons, Michael and Gabriel. Their eyes remained fixed on Simon, waiting for his reaction.

An early version of this chapter appeared in Christopher Lyke, ed., *Our Best War Stories: Prize-Winning Poetry and Prose from the Col. Darron L. Wright Memorial Awards* (Johnston, Iowa: Middle West Press, 2020).

All business, Simon strode to the chalk bucket in the corner of the garage, scooped up a handful, and clapped a puff into the autumn air. One hundred eighty gymnast-lean pounds of unimpressed sixteen-year-old.

I twisted down the volume on whatever hip-hop foolishness them boys had going and tried to describe how the way-too-close gunfire pierced the game of bid whist we had going at the rear camp in An Khe that day.

Crack-Crack-Crack. Pause. Then one more. *Crack.*

The black-nylon do-ragged heads bowed around my foot-locker popped to alert. It was my boy Dawk who called it.

"That's an M-16."

I dropped my cards and rushed to the row of Quonset huts along with everyone else. The soldiers Kearns spared—two brothers and an esé—tottered into a clutch with the rest of us, watching the medics cart out three blood-soaked heaps of jungle fatigues on stretchers. Kearns they brought out last— doped to the eyeballs, endotracheal tube taped like a flagpole to the sloppy mass that had been his face, body still quaking in the Dexedrine funky chicken. What is it about certain sons of bitches that makes them so got-damn hard to kill?

"That's it?" Simon asked.

I'd left out the part about sons of bitches, but studying Simon's restless oil-slick dark face, I understood that including that tidbit wouldn't have made any difference.

Michael spoke up. "Not quite the brothers-in-arms shtick you were hoping for, huh, Sy?"

I jerked a thumb at the two forty-five-pound plates on my side of the barbell. "You good with this, Sy?"

"Yeah, leave it, Mr. Frank," Simon answered, a little quicker than he oughta have.

Simon had been my eldest son Michael's best friend for something like five years by then; a near-permanent fixture at my house. Simon shoulda known he wasn't getting some foxhole brotherhood bullshit outta me.

"I ever tell you guys I had to get circumcised after I was drafted?"

"How old were you?" Gabriel asked. My youngest, the writer. Hold on. Actually, in the fall of '96 he was still dancing. That'd put Gabriel at about twelve.

I scissored my fingers in Gab's direction. "Just turned eighteen."

That set the three of them to squirming in their sneakers, hands inching toward nether regions.

"So, circumcision was a condition of your conscription to fight a war for a government that treated you like a second-class citizen?" Michael asked, without pausing for breath.

I chuckled. "Exactly." Over the years I'd referred to getting drafted as a lot of things—mostly as a motherfucker—but never as "conscription."

"The unkindest cut of all," Michael said, shaking his head.

"Julius Caesar." Simon flashed them pearls at Michael. I think I remember every time I saw that boy smile. He was stingy with his grins, like each one cost him fifty bucks and he was on a limited income.

"A'right." I tapped my hand on the barbell. "Enough messing around, Sy. Let's go."

Simon slid under the weight, settling his shoulders onto the bench's leather cushion. He clasped and unclasped his fingers on the perforated steel, then pulled himself eye to barbell and lowered himself back to the bench. Once. Twice. On the third go he popped the weight off the rack with his funky "oohyuhken" grunt—from that Street Fighter video game them boys loved so much. Simon lowered the bar to his chest, then fought it back up. Steady. Machinelike. For a solid set of eight. Two more than I'd got. I guess that Vietnam hair the boy had had up his ass all morning was good for something.

"Oh, I see you angling for a title shot, huh, youngblood?" I said, twisting my trunk in an exaggerated torso stretch.

All three laughed at that.

As a deputy warden over at Antoine State Prison I hadn't done a forced cell movement in more'n a decade, but I still pushed heavy weights. Or at least tried to. Simon—a three-sport jock who'd left us hoarse from cheering after his eleven catches for 178 yards against Tecumseh last week—had been matching me plate for plate for more than a year by then.

I pointed at Michael's and Gabriel's smirks. "Can either of y'all push that for eight?"

Gabriel piped up, "Mom named us for angels, Dad, not dwarves. You know dwarves get a . . ."

"A bonus on their strength score," I interrupted.

Michael and Gabe had my caramel complexion and good looks but not my stocky frame. They used that dwarf joke on me a lot. I didn't mind. Besides, them two brainiacs preferred my Sunday morning gospel of steel to the fire and brimstone they got every time their mother dragged them down to New Hope Baptist.

"Hold up. Hold up," Simon said, leaning over his knees on the bench and pointing at the stereo. "Turn up that Tupac joint."

Michael obeyed, and all three listened in silence to what sounded to me like an X-rated Saturday morning cartoon jingle. Tupac. That boy with all them frivolous tattoos. Like an affair, ink is something a man should only do if it really means something.

"This guy getting shot is a big deal, huh?" I said, indicating with my fingers for Michael to lower the volume a bit.

Michael twisted the knob, plopped cross-legged next to the stereo on the cobalt-gray gym mat, and looked up at me. "Do you remember when Marvin Gaye died, Dad?"

"Vaguely."

"Well, I remember it. You were washing the car. Mom came running outside with the news. You said, 'Jesus,' then sat on the curb."

"How old were you then?" I asked, starting the math in my head.

Michael blinked twice. "Five. But I remember. You sat there awhile."

I grunted and restrained my smile as Michael turned the volume back up. What would I have done with my life if I'd had half them boys' brains?

Sy bounced from the bench to his feet. He leaned over, touched his toes—chest pressed to his thighs—and held. Tough, smart, and strong. If somebody had dealt me that boy's hand, I woulda thrown mine in.

I sure as hell wouldn't have enlisted. That's for got-damn sure.

⚘

At work the next Saturday, Ettie sat on the opposite end of my tan metal desk watching me thumb through her "Prison Rape Elimination Plan."

"You know what the COs are saying about this PREP stuff, right?"

"I can guess," Ettie said.

"Install liquid soap dispensers in the showers."

Ettie, perched like some kinda Ethiopian goddess in my burnt-orange-carpeted office, looked at me.

"You know." I met her gaze for the punch line. "That way no one can drop the soap."

Ettie, unsmiling, tucked a braid behind her ear. "That's actually pretty good."

I hadn't cracked that PREP folder all week and she could definitely tell.

"Did you speak to Simon?" Ettie asked.

Something else I hadn't done.

"Yeah." I paused. "Kind of."

"What's that mean?"

"Means I think the boy has his mind made up regardless of what I tell him."

"Did he tell you," Ettie asked in that cadence black women reserve for speaking to trifling motherfuckers, "that his father died on Tuesday?"

I musta seen Sy half a dozen times since our weightlifting session last weekend. He hadn't said a thing. Jesus. Sixteen years old and that boy carried himself like Jim Brown in the fourth quarter.

"I've never talked to Simon about his father. He never brought him up. Besides, I didn't want to give the impression I was trying to take his dad's place."

"News flash, Frank." Ettie waited for me to meet her eyes. "You filled that void a long time ago."

"You said Simon never met him. His father, I mean."

"Never. And now he's gone, same as Simon's grandfather."

Ettie had a prison marriage followed by a prison divorce. It's a lot more common than people think. She had already been counseling at Antoine for a few years when I started there in

'76, a year after I got my DD-214. Now she ran counseling programs for the whole state, which meant that sometimes—like today—she worked Saturday evenings too.

I pinched the ridge of my nose. "Troy, right?"

Ettie nodded.

Actually, I'd had no trouble at all remembering the name. Troy. The guy Ettie had constantly been shuttling back and forth from California to see back when I was still single. I'd looked at Ettie differently back then, but nothing had ever come of it. And now I had a wife, a family, and a job in management; I loved the first two, didn't hate the last. More than all that, though, I depended on Ettie mentoring my boys. Hell. Michael had been in junior high when Claire and I gave up on trying to keep up with his reading.

"We'll be going down to New Orleans for the funeral. Simon will meet some of his father's . . ." Ettie scanned the off-white stucco wall behind me before deciding on "colleagues."

"Panthers?" I asked.

"Former Panthers." She smiled tightly. "I talked to Claire a couple hours ago."

Damn. Ettie was pulling out all the stops; she knew full well that even after all these years, my wife had never fully warmed to her. Claire the red-boned, processed-hair, we-shall-overcome church girl and Ettie the headwrap-wearing, Angela Davis–spouting ideologue who wasn't passing anybody's paper-bag test. Claire accepted Ettie like she did my night shifts: something you tolerated for decent health insurance. And Ettie knew it. But Simon—as calloused as he was to the world—never failed to make Claire laugh, probably more than she wanted to. And Ettie knew that too.

"Claire and I agreed that you need to talk to Simon before we head down to New Orleans. He's on the cusp, Frank. Him and Michael. They'll be seventeen in a couple weeks. Old enough for the military's delayed-entry program. The decisions those two make this year are biggies."

"I don't think Michael is too interested in the military."

Ettie laughed a little too loud at that. "You think?"

The boys did spend just about as much time at her house as they did at mine. Ettie was notorious for breaking up summertime Super Nintendo marathons with mandatory thirty-minute reading breaks.

"I don't know what to tell that boy about the military. Even when I first got back, I never talked about Vietnam much. Decreases the chance of someone pissing me off."

That excuse sounded even more pathetic than the shit about not wanting to replace Simon's father. Everybody knows someone who'd fought in Vietnam and didn't want to talk about it. Still, I figure it's better than being one of those guys who never shut up about Vietnam, the ones who saw themselves as the true victims of the war. Everybody knows one of them guys too.

"Tell him the truth," Ettie said.

The prison's public announcement system screeched to life, startling both of us. "Code Red, Wing Two! Code Red, Wing Two!"

Ettie smoothed her pants against her thighs. "Should I wait in my office?"

Ettie and I had worked together in the Oklahoma Department of Corrections for more than twenty years. Long enough for her to know that, whether this was an assault on a correctional officer, a fight between inmates, or a medical emergency, as a counselor her role was, for now, to get outta the way.

I stood up behind my desk. "Give me an hour or so to sort this out." I tapped a finger on the PREP folder. "I know this is important. We'll discuss it, okay?"

Ettie's gaze dropped to her watch. I glanced at the wall-mounted clock behind her. Eighteen thirty already.

"Let's do it Monday." Ettie stood. "Don't make me have to track your sorry ass down again, Frank." She placed a hand on her hip. "Good to go?"

"Good to go." I repeated, smirking. "And I'll talk to Simon. Really talk to him."

I hauled ass for leather down the stairs of the staff wing, across the reception area, and up to the thick glass of the control room. Measmer, a gangly, blond former coastguardsman fresh out of the academy, leaned into the VHF radio base station, pen poised over a blank notepad.

I drummed my fingers on the glass, caught the youngster's eyes, and pointed to the door.

"Oh shit. Sorry, Warden," Measmer mouthed. He walked to the 1950s-style control panel and buzzed me in.

"What do we got?" I asked.

"Not sure, Warden. Nestor's in charge in Wing Two today."

We exchanged a look. Measmer got it. A good kid. One of the best to come out of that class.

"None of them have gotten on the horn yet to confirm what's going on. Nothing on the CCTV either." Measmer gestured to the row of TV screens flickering between black-and-white views of empty stairways, hallways, and rec rooms.

"Try Nestor again," I said.

Measmer keyed the VHF handset. "Whiskey Tango One, this is Charlie Romeo."

The handheld on my hip squawked from proximity to the base station. I twisted the knob on the device to turn down the volume.

"Charlie Romeo, this is Whiskey Tango One." Nestor's voice, giddy with excitement, crackled through the VHF speaker. "Alert Delta Whiskey One that he needs to come up here."

Measmer looked at me.

"Tell him I'm coming up," I said.

Measmer spoke into the handset, "Copy that. Delta Whiskey One en route." Then to me: "Want me to go up with you, Warden?"

"What? And abandon your post?" I placed my hand on Measmer's shoulder. "Hold down the fort here."

Measmer buzzed me through to the prisoner side of the facility.

My corfams echoed in the deserted hallway, their glossy shine reflecting the dull glow of the wall-mounted emergency lights—that dim amber twenty-four-hour reminder of incarceration. I bounded up the ladder well to Wing Two and punched the buzzer, mind tight with that rush I learned to sorta love and sorta hate during the war.

Nestor swung open the steel door. Physically, he wasn't a punk. Nestor stood well over six feet and had proved on prisoners' bodies just how much of his bulk he could transform into brute force. But he was still a coward.

Nestor began speaking before I could even step in, his tone that of a tattling schoolboy. "Riggs threatened me from his cell. He's got a shank. Now he's demanding to talk to you." He waited a good five seconds before adding, "Warden."

I gave him a look that could have reshaped iron. "Let me in, Nestor."

Two standing fans oscillated hot air and the smell of disinfectant around the taut, windowless space. Eight COs suited in react gear—body armor, batons, and shields—stood rattling against each other in the area just before the cellblock, artificial light glinting off their lowered visors. Nestor cocked his head in anticipation of my orders.

If a cartoonist was to sketch a prison guard—exploiting every lame-ass stereotype us COs despise—he would turn out someone exactly like Nestor. The latest accusation of misconduct against the bastard involved instigating a fight between two inmates.

"Did you see those fucking apes going at it?" Nestor had joked in the break room afterward.

Nestor never talked about the event that prompted his transfer from McAlester prison a few years ago. But I heard young COs whisper to one another, "That's him. That's Colin Nestor. Dude broke a con's jaw in Big Mac." Nestor loved that the story had grown legs.

The seasoned COs almost universally disliked Nestor, but they'd back him against a con. The same groupthink compelled soldiers to cover for each other in Vietnam, for everything from curfew violations to rape. But institutional loyalty alone didn't explain the concentrated aggression in front of the cellblock that day. Behind their face shields the COs' eyes pleaded for a "go" order. They wanted to storm a cell and stomp a con. I know the feeling. Hell. I love that rush of fraternal adrenaline as much as the next guy. But as a deputy warden, it was my job to ask questions; and when it came to the Nestors of the world, I had plenty.

"I saw the weapon," Nestor spoke more to the other COs than to me. "Reason enough for a forced cell move to Special Quarters." Long pause. "Warden."

"Shut up, Nestor." I turned to the assembled COs. "Stand fast here. Lemme try talking to him first."

"Roger that, Warden." The COs responded in unison.

I started down the row of cells, a spider of cold sweat crawling down my back. The cellblock reeked of that pitched battle between human excrement and industrial-strength bleach. As a deputy warden, I didn't walk the rows much anymore. The stench I had grown used to while earning my stripes immediately set my heart to thudding in my chest.

A detached voice from behind the bars cursed all creation. "Fuck me. Fuck this. Fuck you."

My gut corded. "It's Warden Mathis, Riggs."

A shank clattered onto the gray tiled floor in front of the cell.

"'Preciate you coming up, Warden," Riggs said. "I know your boys out there are chomping at the bit for a go at me."

I kneeled, picked up the shank, flipped it around in my hand. A toothbrush handle reinforced with electrical tape, sharpened on the end, and spliced with a disposable razor. A nasty little piece of work. Prison and war encourage ingenuity.

I stepped in front of the cell. "What's going on, Riggs?"

Riggs leaned his forehead against the bars. "That bitch-ass Nestor talking about how the last governor granted less than 3 percent of paroles for lifers. Like I don't already fucking know that shit."

As a black, nonsnitching former gangbanger convicted of murder, Riggs occupied the top of the Antoine prisoner hierarchy—a delicate equilibrium of connection, conviction, sexual preference, and race (not necessarily in that order).

I'd known Riggs since I was a rookie CO. Back when I was still walking the yard during rec time, watching sparrows catch a buzz on the electric fence, knowing full well I was within swinging distance of every concealed shank on that patch of grass and concrete—the only part of Antoine that the sun touched. Hell, the better part of both our lives had been more about prison than anything else.

"You pulled the shank to get Nestor to shut up."

"Yeah," Riggs replied.

"You got anything else in there we need to know about?"

"Nah."

"You sure? You know my boys are fixing to turn this cell inside out."

"I'm sure, Warden."

"Relax, Riggs. They'll do their search and that'll be it. No one's going to pursue this." I slipped the shank into my cargo pocket. "Try to get some sleep. We'll have the governor's decision in the morning."

Riggs nodded, opened his mouth as if to thank me, but instead squeezed his eyes shut and nodded again.

The governor's denial of Riggs's parole came through bright and early, just after first count.

I stayed on a couple hours after shift to escort Riggs back to gen pop myself. That and to have a couple choice words with Nestor—if he tried to write up Riggs he'd be doing so without any support from me.

By the time I left the facility late Sunday morning all I wanted was to shit, shower, shave, and sleep.

Back at the house, after ticking the first two off my list, I wiped the steam from my bathroom mirror in preparation to enjoy the third. I squeezed a dime-sized portion of shaving cream onto my boar's-hair brush, then splayed the lather across my face to the sounds of Claire fussing over church clothes in our bedroom. I reached over my head with my left hand, pulled the cheek tight, and slid the razor along my face in short, smooth strokes. A proper shave. Ain't nothing quite like it.

If memory serves, it was later that same year that I demonstrated the process to the boys. When I flicked out my straight edge, Simon looked me dead in the eyes, serious as a heart attack, and said, "That is so fucking badass, Mr. Frank." Setting the four of us to giggling like schoolgirls.

I got my first proper shave at Am Tinh's, the spade whorehouse outside the base camp in An Khe. Back in '71, the GI version of tolerance didn't extend to getting laid. Shit. Probably still don't. The white boys hocus-pocused some of the Vietnamese whores into Sally Annes and viciously protected their investment. Meanwhile, the fiercest black cats made sure that only down white boys set foot in Am Tinh's.

"Trust me, youngblood," my best friend Dawk told me, sitting on his bunk and running the saw edge of his Swiss Army knife through his mustache. "Joint's got the best juke box in 'Nam."

I chose Qui, a "mama-san" in her maybe late twenties, which put her a decade ahead of me. Had myself half-convinced that choosing Qui was some kind of enlightened decision on account of her age. Truth told, those teenage whores—with faces hardened by nights of straight liquor and closed fists— terrified me. 'Course, Qui frightened my nineteen-year-old ass too, but she was older, and somehow that made the whole arrangement seem okay. It took getting home to realize just how unrecognizable my wartime caveats had rendered my morals. That's the thing: when you go to war, your soul is at as much hazard as your body. More really.

Still, I'd be lying if I didn't admit how much I savored those nights at Am Tinh's. The baths that never quite washed off the exhaustion and fear, the saffron-tinged breeze flapping the floor-length vanilla curtains, those deep purple and cotton-candy-pink sunsets through the glassless windows, drifting off to sleep with Qui bent over me like a human orchid. And that's exactly how I'd treated her: like an ornament. Her English was good, but I was having the first steady sex of my life and hadn't really been listening. Qui had mentioned a mother. A sister. A village.

"The people surrender to whoever is there. When the VC came, we surrendered. When the Americans came, we surrendered. If the NVA come, we will surrender." Here Qui smiled, ran her hand through hair so black it stole the light. "That is how we survive."

In the mirror, I noticed Claire watching me.

"How long you been there?"

"Long enough to know your mind is someplace else." Claire raised a manicured eyebrow. "Ettie called last night."

"Man. She is in a full-court press."

"Can you blame her?"

I met Claire's gaze in the bathroom mirror. It took a lot for her to say that. All these years and Claire still manages to surprise me.

"The boys are down in the basement," Claire said. "All ready for you to get them out of morning service so y'all can lift."

"I'm gonna talk to them." I glided the straight edge over my cheek. "All three of 'em."

Number four on my to-do list was gonna have to wait.

Claire nodded, watching her reflection as she adjusted the lace doily pinned to her hair.

"New church crown?" I winked, holding the blade under the tap.

Claire nudged her shoulder into my back. "This one I've had for years."

I headed to the couple bottles I kept tucked in the corner of the "good" living room, the showpiece that Claire never allowed any of us to actually sit in. I filled half a glass with Crown Royal, then lifted it to my nose with both hands and let the scent warm my lungs. I topped off the glass with soda water. All them rules about drinking in the morning go out the window once you start working shifts. Hell. I deserved a drink before this conversation.

I caught up with the boys in my basement, watching BET.

"Hey, guys."

Simon gave me a thumbs-up from his usual spot on the floor, head propped up on a sofa pillow. "Hey, Mr. Frank."

Michael and Gabriel nodded to me from the couch.

I lowered myself onto the recliner, setting my glass on the armrest and missing the days when sitting down didn't require so much effort.

"I want to talk to y'all about the army."

Simon, cradling his knees between his elbows, rocked himself to a seated position.

"Come on." Michael tapped Gabriel's leg. "Let these two indulge their fascist side."

My sons stood up, and Simon made a play swipe at Michael's leg.

"No." I pointed at the remote control and Simon clicked off the TV. "I want you two to stay."

Michael and Gabriel exchanged shrugs, then settled back onto the couch.

I took a breath.

"Most of the fighting I was involved in took place in Cambodia. That probably don't mean a whole hell of a lot to you guys now. But it meant we fought more NVA than Viet Cong. North Vietnamese regulars. Professionals. Real soldiers, like us.

"The heavy contact went down about ten or fifteen miles over the border. I can count those times on one hand. I was shitting myself with fear every time. I spent that entire year terrified and exhausted. Hell, sometimes the only reason I didn't make a run for it was because I was just too got-damned tired." I paused, looked at Simon. "You'd handle it better." I waved off his protest. "Nah. You would. But there was something else too. Kind of like getting off. Like an orgasm, when you thought you smoked one."

That last bit was embarrassing. But how do you express it? That war is hell, but at its height it's also life. Life multiplied by some number no one's heard of yet.

"Mostly we shot farm animals though. Pigs, chicken, oxen . . ."

"Why?" Simon asked.

"Some villages were suspected of supporting the enemy. Hell, the only reason I carried my zippo was to burn hooches. I didn't even smoke."

Fragile, ancient things, them villages. Without hardly putting our minds to it, we'd decimate even the big ones in a single afternoon. The whole company—a hundred-plus grunts—watching flames take shape on thatched roofs in the midday sun. My nineteen-year-old mind figuring that surely this many people wouldn't expel this much effort on something wrong, would they?

Then the sergeants would form us up, and we'd drag ass on. Flamethrower heat from them smoldering huts at our backs, women's screams ringing in our ears, usually without a single VC in tow, and me so fucking exhausted that, as far as judgment went, I might as well have been piss drunk.

"What do you mean, 'when you thought you smoked one'?" Gabriel asked.

"You could never really be sure."

I didn't know shit from apple gravy when I first showed up. Under ambush, I aped the guys in my platoon and sent rounds downrange. *Ta-tat-tat-tat-tat-tat-tat.* Like the air was alive with lead. Looking back, I'm pretty sure something would have shifted inside me if I'd actually killed someone. I would've known. But I didn't tell the boys that. I didn't wanna cop outta what I might've done.

"My first squad leader was a lot like you, Simon. Dawkins. Terrell Dawkins. Tough motherfucker. All gas, no brakes. Always volunteering to walk point." I shook my head, smiled. "Sniper bait. When I first met him, I thought he was nuts."

I tried to describe Dawk during that first meeting. Sitting on a rock, face two hollow cheeks with a thick nugget of a nose in between, flipping the selector switch on his weapon back and forth between semi and full while staring off into the bush like some crazy Zulu tribesman. Take your average understrength infantry company—one hundred spics, spades, and white trash. Ten shouldn't be there. Eighty are just targets. Ten do the fighting and, if you're lucky, one of these is a gotdamned savage. That was Dawk. In a cadre of touched men Dawk's mania stood out, making him the platoon superstar.

"Dawk's theory was that the second man was more likely to get hit than the first. The kind of guy who didn't get medals, just that deep field respect that mattered more." I stopped short, reminding myself: no bullshit. "He was a good killer. One of our best."

"Fortune favors the bold," Simon said.

"God smiles on idiots and drunks," Michael shot back.

"I don't know about all that." Those two. Constantly tossing quotes back and forth. "In war you learn more about cowardice than courage. That and luck."

All them crazy superstitious rituals to fool yourself into believing that it wasn't just random. Always volunteering for point. Only smoking on every second break. Never walking in tank tracks. Anything to convince yourself that getting smoked depended on more than just ending up fifth in line on patrol, or where you took a dump, or when you noticed that your bootlaces were untied. War didn't give a shit if you were loved by many or not at all. Charlie was greasing three hundred GIs a month in '71, and every one of their mommas had told them they was special. A reality so fucked up that superstition became the only rational system of belief. It just so happened that Terrell's crazy-ass superstitious rituals gave that motherfucker the confidence to stalk the jungle like an immortal. Boys like Terrell—and Simon—don't need much convincing of their immortality. In my experience, that type fears cowardice more than anything that might actually kill them.

In the bush, Dawk spotted loose soil, crushed foliage, and catgut trip wires. He heard the unnatural silence before an ambush as if possessed of some deeper understanding of these people clawing for survival. Still, on some level we all musta known that part of it was just dumb luck that kept us from getting hit when Terrell was on point. But the fact remained: the men of Third Platoon–Bravo Company–First Cavalry Division didn't get hit when Dawk walked point. Never. Not once. Even on patrols a good ten, fifteen miles into Cambodia. The heart of Indian country. So far out that we was resupplied by mermite cans kicked out the side of a Huey.

"Dawk was already in his second tour when I showed up in the summer of '71. He had something to prove. Usually that made guys dangerous. But not Dawk. I think deep down, Dawk wanted to challenge all the things white boys had been telling him his whole life. He reveled in how them white boys feared, respected, and required his ferocity—out there in the bush searching for something only he wanted to find. After he made staff sergeant, he bucked for a third tour. When my year in country was up, I rotated back to the States and spent the rest of my enlistment at Fort Hood handing out basketballs at the base gym."

I licked my lips and took a sip of my Crown and soda.

"Terrell and me used to talk a lot about Black National-ism. How the war in Vietnam was going to change everything for the black man in the United States. He once asked me what niggers had done when they returned from America's other wars." The boys winced. I guess that word grated outta my mouth, but not Tupac's. I plowed ahead. "They'd kept on being niggers. But this time it was gonna be different."

When I was Simon and Michael's age, almost everyone I knew was black. Lieutenant Nic Voivodeanu, the Third Platoon commander, had been my first white friend. Well, as much as a second lieutenant could be a PFC's friend, anyway.

One time in the mess hall in An Khe, Nic spotted me in the middle of scratching out a letter home.

"Who're you writing to, Mathis?" Nic asked.

"My mom, sir."

I returned to my letter, but felt the LT still there, examining the top of my head.

"Sir?" I asked, looking up.

"How old are you, Mathis?"

"Nineteen, sir."

Nic grinned. "I bet your parents are proud."

I didn't say how, before leaving for boot camp, my mom made a point of telling me about the battered, castrated body of a black World War II vet swinging from a yellow poplar in her neighborhood back in Tennessee.

"They'd stripped off his uniform before stringing him up," my mom said. She talked about the racism of those days—the everyday terror—without bitterness or self-pity. That's just the way things were.

Nah, I didn't tell my West Point–educated lieutenant that. Instead I nodded and returned the LT's smile. But you best believe I told my boys about that lynching. In the basement that day, I told them boys to love their country. It's the only one we got. You better love it, try to make it better. But don't ever get caught acting like it can't happen. It did. It does.

Nic couldn't understand the rage of the flip-flopped men tracking our platoon in the bush, still less those flip-flopped men's perfect comprehension of us black draftees marching for an empire that didn't want us. The same way a kid like Measmer couldn't see himself pulling a shank on someone like Nestor. They see gooks and cons, where I see men with identities shaped around survival. Men like me, only more desperate and maybe, just maybe, more brave.

"We arrived to Vietnam just two more boys who couldn't get out of that Selective Service letter." I knifed a hand in Michael's direction, unintentionally giving the boy a jump. "Conscripts. But we became volunteers. Every single one of us over there was really a volunteer."

That last bit I said more to myself than to the boys.

"The lieutenant wrote to me at Fort Hood when Dawk finally bought it."

I'm not sure how long it took to medevac Dawk back to the division hospital after he stepped on that manure-tinged punji stick. I do know that once the wound went gangrenous, Dawk was dead in a week. Staff sergeants didn't walk point. Maybe Dawk had been the number two man when the contaminated wood pierced his boot. Nic didn't say.

I wasn't close to all the guys our platoon lost in Vietnam. I watched in silence as PFC Danny Pierce gurgled pink while waiting for a dust off. Doc Reynolds on his knees next to him, fighting all those obscene animal bits leaking outta the hillbilly's punctured body. Exactly a week earlier, Nic had ordered Pierce to remove the Confederate flag he'd draped over his bunk. Nah, I hadn't felt sorrow while Pierce lay there, making the sound of a baby working up the energy for a good scream. Distress and disgust, yeah—same as I'd felt when they'd carted Sergeant Kearns's psychotic black ass outta the mess tent—but not sorrow.

But here's the thing. Losing so many contemporaries— boys like Dawk, Pierce, and Kearns, boys with similar hopes, fears, and families—so early in life wears on your soul in a way that I couldn't articulate. Hell. How do you articulate any of it? How napalm leaves less than bones? The violent beauty of muzzle flashes at night? Growing old in an afternoon?

Friendships cleansed of all that shit that seems so important back in the world? How someone getting killed starts to feel natural. And why shouldn't it? That's the way it's been for most of human existence.

Instead, I maintained an eye contact with Simon that the teenager—as tough as that boy was—just couldn't bear.

"The things that defined my service won't define yours." My gaze settled onto my hands, clasped around my glass. "Kids join the military for a lot of different reasons, Sy. Make sure you're doing it for the right ones."

A week later, Simon attended his father's funeral in New Orleans. Two weeks after that, Simon asked me to drive him to the recruiters' offices.

Ettie wasn't angry, or at least she didn't show me any anger. "He's made his decision," she told me on the phone when they were back from Louisiana. "I'm at peace with it. I'm glad you're going to be with him when he talks to those recruiters."

Throughout all this, Simon didn't mention his dad once. Still hasn't.

"What defined your service, Mr. Frank?" Simon asked as we drove to Antoine's storefront row of recruiting stations, bookmarked by a Blockbuster and a Piggly Wiggly.

I stared at the station wagon's windshield for a couple seconds.

"Violence, race, and drugs."

"Those things won't define my service."

He was probably right. Them boys generally was.

We talked to all four. The marines don't have special forces, the army could guarantee a slot at Ranger School but nothing more, and Simon didn't like the navy's uniforms. While walking between recruiting offices, we got a good laugh outta how

Michael woulda responded to this less than scientific process of elimination. Simon ended up signing a delayed-entry contract with the air force that guaranteed him a shot at pararescue. "The PJ pipeline," the recruiter called it. Special forces right outta the gate. Exactly what Simon wanted.

The boys graduated in the spring of '98 and had one last summer together. In the autumn, Michael packed for Columbia University, Simon for Lackland Air Force Base.

✿

The governor granted Riggs's parole six years later. May 5, 2004, a Wednesday. Measmer, looking sharp and confident with supervisor's pips shining on his collar, walked Riggs downstairs. I watched Measmer and Riggs trading jokes as they passed through the sally port to the staff side. Measmer handed me the manila folder that contained Riggs's file.

I signed the pink release slip paper-clipped to the front of the folder. Then I shook Riggs's hand. In my twenty-seven years at Antoine, this was the third time I personally met a prisoner for release.

Riggs smiled, eyes wide and moist at the edges. "Now for the hard part."

I found Simon sitting in my living room with Ettie, Claire, and Gabriel that evening.

Simon, in ramrod-straight civvies, popped to his feet when I walked in. "Look at you, old man."

I grabbed him and held him way too long in a vain attempt to chokehold the restlessness still pulsating from his body. Be still now, son. Now is the time to be still.

Simon told prepackaged, safe war stories. The constipation from weeks of eating nothing but MREs, the Afghan interpreter who had a penchant for walking on his hands in the nude and whose English was flawless until he cussed. (*Bastard son of cocksucking motherfuck! Yes! You, my friend!*)

"What was his name?" Gabriel asked.

"Who?" Simon said.

"The nudist interpreter."

"Wesley. Wes. He picked his interpreter name because he loved Wesley Snipes movies—*Blade, Passenger 57*, even *Demolition Man*. Dude wouldn't shut up about *New Jack City*." Simon smiled, looked down at the empty coffee cup in his hands. Then he met my eyes. "Wes. All gas, no brakes, that guy."

I heard things that Ettie, Claire, and Gabriel didn't. Things both Simon and I were glad the other understood, but that we wouldn't say aloud. As if we had an unspoken pact not to sully the language of peace with descriptions of war.

Claire cleared the coffee cups from the living room table after the boys left.

From the couch, Ettie and I listened to Claire fussing in the kitchen.

Ettie stood up. "I should help."

"Yeah, me too." Creaking like an old man, I rose from the couch.

"He smiles more," Ettie said.

I nodded, walked to the window, and parted the drapes just in time to see the taillights of Simon's truck disappearing from our cul-de-sac.

You made it, son. Now comes the hard part.

4 | Dancing in Place

Norman, Oklahoma
March 2004

> An artist is a creature of habit. A creature of
> routine. A creature of movement.

I MET DAPHNE at the Whitter Recreation Center in Norman, Oklahoma, where—on Mondays, Wednesdays, and Fridays—I taught modern dance. That's what I called the class anyway, even though it wasn't much more than jazzercise routines brushed over with what my uncles called "highfalutin dance talk."

On the first day, I told the class to call me Mr. Gabriel.

Then, surrounded by Fortress of Solitude reflections of myself in a Chewbacca T-shirt and matching tan tights, I paused, astounded that no one burst out laughing.

I went through a brief introduction. An adagio, a pas de basque, a pirouette, a pas de bourrée. The basic steps. I settled my worn Capezios onto the slatted floor after each movement, twisting the ball of my left foot and bracing on my right heel.

Each time I looked up my eyes found their way back to Daphne. With Choctaw cheekbones, mascara that hinted at a dominatrix streak, and acne scars like cracks in a porcelain doll, Daphne's face wasn't one you forgot. And—I'm just going to go ahead and say it—you didn't forget her tits either. Titans, topped by silver-dollar-sized areolas that prompted a long, hard reevaluation of my sorry-ass life every time I saw them. After quitting competitive dancing in high school and attending a college close enough to do laundry at my parents' place every weekend, a part of me felt I didn't deserve boobs like Daphne's in my life.

Nothing magical happened after I finished my BA. And nothing magical was going to happen if I finished the MA in English literature I was now half-assedly working on. Or when I turned thirty. Or got married. I'd be the same asshole. If anything, I'd be worse. I'd spent the last year of my life penning a fantasy novel as cautiously as possible, using genre as a cover for writing like a coward—horror-stricken by things dark, strange, dangerous, difficult, and deep.

But I did have my "highfalutin" intramural dance class, and I planned to run that bad boy like tryouts for the Bolshoi. By the middle of March, I'd whittled my fourteen students down to seven undergrads and Daphne.

Clap—Clap—Clap. Clap-Clap-Clap. Clap—Clap—Clap.

I paced beside the eight survivors lined up on the bar. My hands picked up the momentum of Al Green's *I'm Still in Love with You* (from his fifth studio album, the one with him all pimped out in an Afro and white leisure suit on the cover). I wanted tendus so swift that calves melded into a blur.

"Shoulders down. Listen to the music."

Clap—Clap—Clap. Clap-Clap-Clap. Clap—Clap—Clap.

My palms stung and the mirrors had fogged by the time Al smoothed out that final crescendo.

The slatted wood creaked as I strode to the CD player in the corner. Sixteen eyes tracked me pleadingly as I bent at the waist and pressed stop.

"First arabesque with the arms. Dégagé those legs derriere. And lift. Straight thighs." Chin aloof and mirrored wall at my back, I held the pose in front of the class. "No shallow breaths."

"Dégagé." I tuned out the silent, collective whimper clotting the stagnant air. "And lift. Stretch those legs. Hold."

"Dégagé." I gave them a few seconds. "Now lift."

By the fifth round, thighs had begun to tremble, but not mine and not Daphne's.

"That's the thing about weakness," I said, stealing a line from Mr. Sergei, my old dance instructor. "Everybody in the studio feels it at once."

Even Daphne, tough as a mare—massive boobs constrained in a skintight black binder—began to grimace.

"Straight legs," I said, then added with the affected scorn instructors reserve for their best students, "Fix your face, Daphne."

Audible breathing, glistening noses, any facial expression— all signs of imperfection. We'll stop when legs refuse to rise. This is how I was taught, the only way I know: There is no justice. It's not fair. Be quiet.

"All this fucking ballet," Daphne mumbled. "I thought this was supposed to be *modern* dance."

The college girls giggled. I'm light skinned enough that they probably saw the heat I felt coursing up my neck.

"Basics reinforce everything else," I said. "Besides, no one asked you to be an artist." Another Mr. Sergei line. Jesus. Did I really say that out loud?

Holding my pose with a face bright as a fresh tomato, I waited for the snickers to intensify.

Instead Daphne solidified her posture. The other girls followed suit. Weakness isn't the only thing everyone in the studio feels at once.

I waited a few beats. "Dégagé."

I snuck a glance at Daphne.

She was staring at her own reflection, not looking at me at all.

"All right," I commanded. "Lift."

After class, I planted my seat bones on the floor, with my back to the mirrored wall, and rotated my feet at the ankle. First the left, then the right.

The girls, congratulating themselves with curt nods, filed out of the studio.

They all had heart; a few even boasted a couple scattered classes here and there: jazz, ballet, tap. Daphne was the closest to decent. None had put in the hours to be good. It takes thousands of hours—stacked one after another like an infinite game of dominoes—to get good. As somebody who quit just a sliver past decent, I should know.

"Hey." Daphne's voice echoed in the empty studio. "This is your first time teaching, huh?"

"Yeah." Summoning my inner Mr. Sergei, I bricked my face and didn't look up from my toes. "I told you guys that from the get-go."

At twenty-six, Daphne was three years older than me, and half a decade older than her classmates. But she didn't get to question my chops. In places like Antoine, brown boys who danced and played role-playing games suffered for it. I'd taken that shit on the chin every goddamned day in Antoine and still managed to place in state and national dance contests as a teenager.

Dancing had meant a bizarre adolescence—no booze, no drugs, no late nights, no real love life. For eight years I poured all my time, energy, and guts into dancing. Eight years. Long enough to have become a doctor. Then, just like that, it was over.

Four-year hiatus between quitting dance after high school and teaching this class be damned; I'd suffered too much in studios just like this one to let Daphne—or anyone—question my chops.

"Easy, tiger." Daphne showed me her palms in surrender. "I'm just asking."

It took every iota of discipline in my body to hold my gaze above the tiny gold cross on her choker.

"I want you to come see my routine at Lil' Darlings tomorrow night," Daphne said.

"Lil' Darlings?" I asked.

"The strip joint where I work." Daphne sighed at the gargantuan burden of disabusing me of my staged ignorance. "I'm a stripper. You knew that."

"I figured you were a dancer." I rose to my feet and placed both palms on my lower back. "Didn't know the specifics."

All of which was true, but at that moment Daphne and I were staring past each other anyway. A pair of dancers fixated on their reflections. Only bodybuilders have a worse relationship with mirrors.

According to Daphne, Lil' Darlings was the minor league of Oklahoma City strip joints.

"Now Baby Dolls," she said, "that place is the majors."

"Is the quality always directly correlated with the creepiness of the name?"

Daphne looked at me. It took a few seconds for me to understand that she was offended on behalf of Baby Dolls—a thought that infused every cell in my heart with pity.

"I don't know," I said. "Tuesday night at a strip joint?"

Daphne's eyes scanned up from my gnarled feet to my meticulously unkempt 'fro and then back down again. Finally, her curled lip eased into the mercy of not calling my bullshit.

Who was I kidding? In the world of strip joints, I didn't know the difference between weeknights, weekends, or holidays (although if forced to guess, I bet the Fourth of July is pretty big at Lil' Darlings). Frankly, Daphne's invitation was the most exciting thing to happen in my life since my undergrad crew had—in all their Atari T-shirted, corduroy-trousered glory—abandoned me for law schools, real jobs, PhD programs, and marriage.

"C'mon, Gabe," Daphne said.

I don't mind "Gabe" or even "Gabs" with friends, but up to this point Daphne was my student. I let this register on my face.

Undaunted, Daphne continued, "Lil' Darlings is packed on the weekends. You won't be able to give me as good a feedback on my routine if I'm scraping tips in front of a full house."

I continued this back-and-forth just long enough for my feigned disinterest to be duly noted.

The following evening, I found myself just off I-35—between Oklahoma City and Norman—sitting at a black-tiled bar topped with advertisements for domestic beer and one of those flashing neon signs of a cabaret dancer kicking up a leg. Seriously.

Was the cabaret dancer sign hung sarcastically? Were the red, green, and blue Christmas tree lights twinkling on the catwalk-style stage meant to give Lil' Darlings a seedy, yet oddly festive, vibe? Was I giving the owner(s) too much credit? Not enough?

I ordered a Budweiser. It seemed the thing to do.

The bartender—blond buzz cut, pierced lower lip, black T-shirt straining against overworked biceps—gave me a surprisingly contempt-free bro nod. Dudes who frequent strip joints alone on Tuesday nights deserve a certain degree of reflexive societal contempt, don't they?

Obscured in a tinted booth next to the stage, the DJ drew scattered applause from the seven or so other patrons. "Gentlemen, let's hear it for Hannah!"

I halfway expected a middle-aged Jewish intellectual. Instead a cadaverous blonde in a glow-in-the-dark thong and three-inch glass heels plodded onto the stage to Radiohead's "Idioteque."

Two stools over, a guy with thick, gray hair blossoming from his ears glanced at the catwalk in the mirror behind the bar, then returned to his curly fries.

Applaud, boo, throw something, but fucking react. I have limped offstage in tears—chest heaving, skin and costume soaked, 'fro deflated in defeat—but at least I've never been ignored during a performance.

I've got to hand it to Hannah though: that girl never stopped moving. About halfway through—around when Yorke's voice bifurcates into that trippy double echo bit—she scaled to the top of the pole and performed an ambitious (if somewhat inelegant) fairy-sit down to the stage.

A couple good ole boys in an identical uniform of skintight jeans and frayed baseball caps gave halfhearted whoops and then tucked folded bills into the fluorescent elastic just above Hannah's Auschwitz hips.

I applauded into the mirror. Hannah had fiercely refused to be rendered nonexistent. I looked around the bar and decided that this was the principal challenge in this place.

The DJ swung impressively from deep cut alternative tracks to '90s neo-soul and back again. I noticed during which acts the customers went for a piss, and when they sat up. Success had something to do with the dancers' builds, but not as much as I'd presumed.

Every group has its biases, and for dancers—who are generally uneducated, apolitical, and amoral—it is the close, sustained, and unhealthy attention we pay to bodies. We dancers casually speak of goddesses, otherworldly figures, clavicles that could contain oceans. Bodies are the first thing our hypercritical eyes notice, and we describe them with a reverence that reflects an inhuman ideal.

When Daphne finally took the stage—to Aretha Franklin's "Natural Woman"—the sultry heft of her curves startled me. As did her athleticism.

With ferocious grace, Daphne pirouetted into a sudden (and overtly suggestive) squat. She danced with a gaze as detached as a junkie questioning the heavens. Not really my thing. This was her room. I wanted her in it. I wanted her to own it.

Aretha belted out the final refrain. *You make me feel!* Daphne ran her palm up the steel pole in the center of the catwalk. Hair draped between her shoulder blades and foreleg wrapped around the pole, Daphne—for the first time that night and for just a half second—struck a fully self-possessed pose. A perfect ratio of hips, lips, and fingertips.

I sipped my beer but didn't taste it.

I imagined plastering those thick, powerful—real—thighs to the sheets, reaching down urgently to squeeze with both hands, and pounding hard. My erection muscled against my jeans. I wanted to fuck with an intensity I'd never felt before.

The word "fuck" had never suggested itself to me in this manner, and that I thought it now—so purely and completely—at first thrilled and then terrified me. An unfamiliar beast, snorting down my neck with something sickeningly close to hatred. Dancing had so narrowed my definition of beauty that I actually despised some of the body types I found most desirable.

Hannah took a seat a couple stools over; her presence jostled me back into the bar.

I turned to her and without thinking said, "Nice set."

Hannah gave me a look like a butter knife—dull and hard.

My face grew hot. I hazarded a laugh.

She left me on the hook for a couple beats before finally saying, "Thanks."

Daphne stepped off the stage and shrugged into a sequined lavender robe from a row of pegs next to the DJ booth—the kind of Victoria's Secret getup I imagined housewives received from their husbands once a year. She smiled in my direction.

"Fresh face." Hannah, suddenly relaxed, slid onto the stool next to me. Her hand met mine on top of the bar. "Not much of a rind on you. How about a lap dance?"

Hannah's big, unembarrassed smile made me smile back.

"How long have you been doing this?" I asked.

"What?" Hannah flipped her limp blonde hair to one side. "Exotic dancing?"

"Exotic dancing?" Daphne wedged into the space between me and Hannah. "Bitch, please. We're strippers. Get good at it."

Hannah showed Daphne a French-tipped middle finger.

"He's with me." Daphne's eyes flashed—vicious out of necessity, but not betraying any particular emotion about it. "Fuck. Off."

Hannah applied herself to conversation elsewhere.

Daphne draped an arm on my shoulder and whirled into the bar stool on my opposite side, a couple spaces from the guy with the hair growing out of his ears.

"Wow. Can't leave you alone for a second, huh, kiddo? So? What do you think?"

"This place is absolutely remarkable," I replied, regretting it immediately. I just couldn't help myself. I felt like a researcher examining some bizarre petri dish of human behavior.

"I meant about my routine." Daphne lifted her chin in the bartender's direction and pointed to my Budweiser.

"Actually, could I get a soda water with a splash of Crown?" Maybe appropriating Frank's drink (and line) would awaken some of my old man's legendary cool. It certainly couldn't hurt.

"Make that two, Alois."

"Are you done for the night?" I asked.

"Nah. Still got two more sets."

"How do you manage to dance while you drink?"

"Practice."

The guy with the soul-patch ears snorted and then stretched, revealing a sliver of pale white belly beneath his Houston Oilers T-shirt.

"So?" Daphne repeated. "My routine?"

"Not bad." Daphne knew I don't dispense "not bads" lightly. I raised my beer, remembered how much I didn't want it, and proceeded to lose any cool I had left by awkwardly replacing the bottle on the bar. "I've got some ideas."

"Yes!" Daphne hissed, balling up her fists in excitement.

"You think too much on stage. Listen and react. No thought is needed." That was Mr. Sergei verbatim, vaguely military syntax and all.

Daphne nodded. She was ready to get to work. The energy crackling between us wasn't sexual, but creative. A hell of a buzz.

Alois placed our drinks on the bar. The guy with the soul-patch ears had finished his curly fries and was now picking through a Styrofoam container of hot wings. Completely bald, the man had thin, barely perceptible eyebrows. The same with his lashes. It was as if his hair had given up everywhere but his ears.

I lowered my voice. "What type of person eats in a strip joint?"

Daphne placed a hand on my thigh, leaned into my earlobe, and whispered, "The hungry type."

I inhaled the heady scent of sweat and perfume. My erection hurt.

Still gnawing on a chicken bone, Soul Patches addressed Daphne as if I were invisible. "What's a fella gotta do to get your number, sweetheart?"

"Weeeeeeell, I could give it to you." Daphne lifted her hand from my thigh and placed it on my shoulder. "But after my father, the thought of getting fucked by another white man kinda grosses me out."

Soul Patches tossed a chicken bone into the Styrofoam container on the bar, dabbed his fingers on his tongue, and then dried them on a napkin. He rose from his bar stool, withdrew several bills from his wallet, and dropped them on the counter. Then he walked out. The whole process took forty seconds or so, during which the man seemed neither surprised nor insulted.

Daphne's shoulders sank an inch after he left.

I didn't even want to know if that story about her father was true. I was just glad that my dick had finally shriveled. Simon, the self-appointed Gangster of Love, used to say that a man with an erection loses 75 percent of his capacity for rational thought. Maybe. But you'd still have to question the soul attached to an erection that could withstand the type of revelation Daphne had just dropped. The last five minutes had left me scared shitless of sleeping with her, even—especially—if my dick felt differently about the matter.

But, man, did I want to chisel the glimmers of beauty out of Daphne's routine. In my gut, I was still much more interested in the challenge of dancing than that of writing, and Daphne felt like a last shot at something. What exactly, I wasn't sure. But something.

And don't try to tell me twenty-three is too young for last shots; dancers might confront the stark reality of mediocrity younger than most, but that doesn't mean they handle it any better.

✿

In addition to the regular modern dance classes, Daphne and I began meeting at Whitter on Tuesdays and at the club (as the employees called it) on Thursdays.

Whether you find stripping cheap and tacky, wild and subversive, stupid, stimulating, offensive, fantastical, one-dimensional, scary, feminist, sexist, sexy, off-putting, amusing, or deadly serious, getting good at it—I mean really good at it—requires just as much time, thought, and energy as any other art form.

At the club, Daphne took me through a brief introduction. The hooks: front, ankle, and knee. The climb and fireman down. From there to the carousel, the Peter Pan, and fairy-sit. The stag. Reverse stag. Scissor-sit. Tabletop. The basic steps.

"Okay." I smiled, felt at home. "Again, from the top."

I worked Daphne from excruciating pain to complete numbness, and she never so much as whimpered. Daphne complained about the blackheads she got from rolling on Lil' Darlings' filthy stage, about the moral shortcomings of her coworkers, about the clear, plastic stickies the state of Oklahoma required her to wear over her nipples—but not once about the dancing itself. That was the job, and Daphne approached getting good at it with a blue-collar work ethic that the artist in me couldn't help but admire. Plus, she paid me for my time—both in the studio and at the club. I ended up wanting Daphne to be a great stripper almost as much as she wanted it for herself.

By my fourth visit, Alois began calling out upon spotting me at the door.

"Gabs! Crown and soda?"

"You know it."

I promised myself to remember Alois in my will.

For the first time since high school I felt fully awake.

I'd begun taking more meals at Daphne's one-bedroom apartment just outside Norman than I did at my own place. I made a point of jerking off before showing up but honestly needn't have bothered—nothing she did or said in my presence was meant to entice.

About a month in, in mid-April, I was hanging at Daphne's when she casually mentioned a boyfriend who'd wanted to eat her feces. Midway through her scatological tale, Daphne paused to belt out the crescendo of the gospel song blaring from the CD player in her kitchen.

"Loooooord! Yes you are! You are! More than liiiiiife to me! Ohhhhhhh. More than life to me." She sang the way she danced: punching fearlessly through the tough bits.

The song ended and she continued talking without a hint of irony in her voice. "He said he wanted to ingest every part of me. Can you imagine?"

"I'd prefer not to."

But try as I might, I did. It occurred to me that the sentiment behind her ex's request was really some beautiful shit. Not beautiful enough to make me forget that what we'd been talking about was eating actual shit, but still.

Stoned, she once told me that a woman must become a mother or a prostitute to get to "the real heart of things." A statement I found equal parts intriguing, baffling, and—as with all Daphneisms—deeply disturbing.

As with the tale of her father, I was dying for the particulars but never asked. That girl oozed sex stories, but—terrified of the grim reality they might drip—I decided it was best not to pick at them too much.

Besides, Daphne told me enough unprompted. Who else could she tell this stuff to? The fellow strippers she detested? The high school buddies whose weddings and baby showers she ignored? Her mom?

Daphne made an already isolating profession more so with a quasi-religious code of morality that made sense only to her. "The skanks" at work took money outright, while Daphne accepted only gifts, dinners, and getaways. Besides maybe her regular church attendance, I could discern no other difference between Daphne's behavior and that of "the skanks."

"I wouldn't give a nickel for any of them bitches," she said. At moments like these you'd get a glimpse of how much loss and regret Daphne hid in her eyes.

As far I was concerned, both Daphne and "the skanks" all swam in the same sexual deep end of three-ways, restroom hookups, and rodeo weekends that began with a former state senator tipping his Stetson and ended with nostriling up behind the old Bolivian marching powder in the Oklahoma City Hilton.

"There's something extra satisfying about persuading a man who thinks you're trash to spend his time and money on you. Preferably so much so that in the end they hate themselves." She removed her scrunchie and shook loose a shock of hair matted with sweat. "It's like, who doesn't have any self-respect now, motherfucker?"

Dangerous waters, with no lifeguards. I resolved not to stray from the shallow end.

❀

At the beginning of May, I attended a graduate student forum convened by a company hiring English instructors for the Bladoonsky Language Institute in Ukraine.

Daphne read over my shoulder as I flipped through the Bladoonsky brochure at her apartment. In the brochure, an Asian American girl flashed a hundred-watt grin at a classroom of

Harry Potter–uniformed Slavic kids with elbows near snapping in apparent eagerness to be called upon.

Daphne read the caption in the Valley girl voice we normally reserved for imitating the undergrads in dance class. "I absolutely melted when my students in Kyiv christened me 'Mashinka,' the Russian diminutive of my name."

"I know." I flipped the page in the brochure and rolled onto my back on her bed. "Corny stuff, right?"

"Your Sergei was from there, right?"

"He studied in Kyiv," I said, surprised Daphne bothered to remember. Usually she talked about the rest of the world in the "us" and "them" parlance of evangelicals for whom heaven and hell were more tangible locations than anywhere outside the Bible Belt. "But he was born in some little town near Odessa."

At the beginning of my first lesson—I must have been ten—Sergei struck a stance in front of our class, chin held with cervine grace, thighs pure sinewy brawn in his tights, every bit as much athlete as artist.

"You can call me Mr. Sergei."

At that moment, I understood that dance isn't cute. At its best it's powerful. At its pinnacle, brutally so.

After class, he introduced himself to my mother as "Sergio," the equivalent of someone named "Mikhail" referring to himself as "Michael." Which just goes to show how little Sergei understood Americans like Claire when he first arrived on a teaching fellowship at Oklahoma City University thirteen years ago.

"A real Soviet dancer!" my mother marveled, driving our wood-paneled station wagon back to our house in Antoine. "Just like Rudolf Nureyeaaa . . ." Claire's voice faded into a trail of indistinct vowels.

"My God! You're like stampeding elephants!" Sergei's English contained no trace of an accent until he raised his voice—which happened often in the studio. Then *God* became *Gad* and he overemphasized the *ele* in *elephants*.

Upon discovering the size of Antoine, Sergei commiserated, "Small towns are like large, uncongenial families, aren't they?"

He wasn't wrong.

But whenever Sergei mentioned Kyiv, I saw a black-and-white snow-dusted amalgamation of Moscow, Prague, and Paris. Places I—a small-town Oklahoma boy—had never visited but imagined to be brimming with intellectuals, radicals, and artists living in the sort of romantic poverty that bred great culture.

Ms. Ettie didn't help, fueling my nascent Russophilia with a steady supply of Akhmatova, Chekhov, and all the rest.

One summer afternoon when I'd been lurking around her driveway, waiting for Simon to get his ass in gear, Ms. Ettie hollered me over to the screen door.

I hightailed it to the porch.

Ms. Ettie pushed open the door with her hip and tossed me a copy of *Hadji Murat* stamped ANTOINE STATE PRISON. "Maybe you can figure out that Russian soul everybody's always talking about."

On Daphne's cream-colored bedspread, my mobile buzzed to life. I didn't recognize the number.

"Hello?"

"Gabs!"

"Who is this?" I asked.

"Who do you think, motherfucker!"

"Sy!" Simon. The only person in my life who regularly and affectionately referred to me as "motherfucker."

"One sec." I held a finger up to Daphne, walked onto the porch, and parked it on the concrete steps leading to her screen door. A canary-yellow plastic bag flapped on the fence at the end of the parking lot. The sky had dimmed to a bruised purple.

"Where are you, man?" I asked. "Michael told me he was expecting you a couple weeks ago."

"I'm in Antoine. I could only camp out on your brother's couch in New York for so long."

"Nice! How long are you in town for?" I cradled the phone between my ear and shoulder, hugging my knees to my chest despite the warm evening air.

"Not sure." His voice shrugged. "I start at Georgetown in January. International relations."

"Ahhhhh, international relations. The manliest of the humanities."

"The manliest of the social sciences. Humanities is for pussies, Mr. English Lit."

I laughed. Only Simon would rate academic fields according to testosterone. "What happened to the air force, the least manly of the military services?"

Simon snorted over the line. "More evidence of just how much us PJs need a movie. Can you imagine what *Black Hawk Down* did for recruiting into the Ranger Regiments?"

"It was a book before it was a movie."

"Yeah. A book that I've read and that I'm about ninety-nine point motherfucking nine, nine, nine, nine sure that you haven't."

"Annnnnd you can go get fucked."

Simon burst out laughing, and then I did too, and my god did it feel good.

"No. But seriously," I said when I caught my breath. "You're done with all that special ops stuff?" If ever there was a person born for that sort of balaclavaed GI Joe shit, it was Simon.

"Done. EASed after my last deployment."

Michael had related bits and pieces of Simon's last tour in Afghanistan. This was lightning-rod territory for the three of us. Still, I was curious how Simon would describe his stints in Bush's wars.

"Decompressing until I start school in the winter," he continued. "That's like a year of nonmilitary fucking around." Simon's voice went flat, then perked back up. "What are you doing tonight, Gabs? I'm bored out of my mind here. Starting to think that deferring Georgetown until January was a mistake."

"Well that's a given," I said, and turned to find Daphne standing behind the screen door, shoulders lurching and mouth flapping in imitation of me trying to be cool. It was actually pretty funny.

I told Simon I'd be out to Antoine in an hour to pick him up, and snapped my mobile closed.

"*The* Simon?" Daphne asked, creaking open the screen door until it nudged my butt crack.

"Dude!" I complained.

Daphne laughed.

"That's the happiest I've ever heard you," she said.

"Yeah?"

"Yeah. I'm dancing tonight. Bring him to the club."

❀

I pulled up to Ms. Ettie's place as the last strands of dusk frayed Antoine's horizon. It'd be dark in a few minutes.

Simon threw open his mother's door, sprinted across the lawn, and snatched me into the air in a tackle-hug.

"Gabs!"

"Hey, Sy."

"Man, look at ya!" He grabbed my cheeks and held my face at arm's length, grinning far beyond the moment when it became awkward.

My gaze dropped to the pavement "Still built like an Olympic sprinter, I see."

"You kidding?" Simon released my face and thumped his midsection. Despite a month's worth of stubble and an untucked polo shirt, his look was as persistently orderly as ever. Simon was like Frank that way; both had bearings that reacted to slovenliness like white blood cells to an infection. "This is the worst shape I think I've ever been in. Your brother made it his mission to keep me drunk the last month."

"Just like I'm fixing to get you drunk tonight, bruh!" I said, hoping that wasn't laying it on too thick. Suddenly I'm back in junior high, hoping Michael's cool new friend would like me. "But first, you know my folks are gonna want to see you."

"A'ight, bet."

A'ight, bet. A line that brought me back to high school and could mean either "I agree" or "I'm fixing to whip your ass."

"Yeah, uh. How about we take my ride, though?" Simon said.

I looked from the late-model black truck in the driveway to the ancient Chevy Chevette my dad wrote a seventy-five-dollar check for during my junior year in high school.

"Man. I'll tell you what: Old Mr. Frank got his money's worth on that bucket," Simon said, laughing.

"Still the first thing he asks about when he calls," I said. To be fair, it was a conversational crutch I relied on just as much as Frank did.

Ms. Ettie stepped outside the house in billowy slacks and a sleeveless blouse that accentuated the sinewy cords lashing through those arms of hers.

"Boy, you better get over here and give me a hug."

I rushed into Ms. Ettie's embrace, folded up in the fragrance of whatever essential oil she was using, and remained there for a long time.

"Go ahead," Ms. Ettie said, slapping my face just hard enough to show she cared. "I'll meet y'all there."

In the jigsaw puzzle neighborhood where we grew up, Simon's place was just a couple blocks from ours. These cookie-cutter homes sprouted up in Antoine in conjunction with the nearby state prison of the same name, where my dad was a deputy warden and Simon's mom was a counselor.

During the short drive to my parents' place, Simon asked about people he went to high school with, girls he'd dated, teachers, coaches. If he'd done only a four-year hitch in the air force, Simon would have returned to find more of his peers in similar transitional phases. But he'd extended his contract after 9/11—he wasn't about to miss his war—and seven years post–high school is a long time. Simon was even more stranded than me.

My mom peeked through the living room curtains as we pulled up. She met us in the doorway and was close to bawling by the time she released Simon.

That's my mom.

"Hey, Ms. Claire," Simon said.

My mother gave my arm a squeeze, then turned back to Simon. "Home for good?"

"Out of the military for good anyway," Simon replied. "Discharge papers and all. Starting school in the winter."

"How many years was that?" Claire asked.

"Six years, nine months," Simon answered immediately.

In his head, I bet Simon had it narrowed down to weeks, days, hours. Like prison time, people always seem to recall precisely how long they served in the military.

"Where's Dad?" I asked.

"He'll be getting off shift shortly. I wanted to surprise him."

"Mom. We're going out."

"Oh." Claire jutted her chin in my direction. "This one's suddenly too busy for coffee."

"Yeah. Busy. Like still teaching, doing a Master's, and writing a novel type of busy."

"How's that novel coming, Gabriel?" Claire asked, gesturing us into the house and maintaining an aggravatingly even tone.

Never ask someone working on his first novel how it's coming. Seriously. That shit is just cruel.

"Just fine, thanks. I'm also thinking of taking a job overseas." I hadn't planned to mention anything about the teaching gig in Ukraine; it just kind of tumbled out of my mouth.

Simon raised a hand in my direction. "A coffee sounds perfect, Ms. Claire. Gabs knows we aren't going anywhere until I see Mr. Frank."

I was slouched on the couch pointlessly stirring a black coffee when my dad strolled in.

"Whose truck is that in my driveway?" Frank stopped short in the living room.

My petulance slipped into a grin at how long it took my father to compose himself.

"Look at you, old man," Simon said.

"Simon." Watching the hug my father gave Simon tore at my soul a little. Just a little. "It's good to see you, son."

"It's good to see you too, Mr. Frank."

Even when smiling at us—his boys—Frank's expression remained pressurized. Growing up under Frank was constant prep for a world that would not treat us tenderly, and Simon had absorbed my father's lessons best.

I hadn't seen Frank and Simon together in years, and the physical contrast between the two struck me. My father was so light skinned that people sometimes asked his ethnicity. Frank would answer "Black American" in a tone that did not invite further inquiry. Meanwhile, Simon, black enough to break daylight, had been christened "midnight" by the meathead athletes who idolized him in high school. But he was always just "Sy" for Michael and me, his real friends. He was always just Sy to us.

"Afghanistan twice," my father said. "Got-damn."

"The military I joined in '98 isn't the one I just left." Simon sounded like he used that line often.

"Draftees like me had it easier than you boys today," Frank said. "We did our one tour and that was it. Then, one way or another, you went home. No one was talking about sending you back for a second or third round."

Simon caught me rolling my eyes. I didn't care.

I grew up listening to my father and uncles talk about the Vietnam War like it had been some wellspring of secret masculine knowledge, as opposed to a colossal fuckup. One of those uncles—when he wasn't discussing life with a surety unavailable to us mere mortals—would, with my father out of earshot, flick his wrists limply and ask, "How's the dancing?"

That had been my introduction to black masculinity's rigid confines of expression. Now don't get me wrong, this was a lesson I needed. I'm glad I got it early. But to get it like that, in your own family, hurt. I'd cut off my pinky for the opportunity to tell Uncle Terrence's two-sips-from-alcoholic ass that now. And now here were Simon and Frank having their own little coded "man talk." Fuck me. The way I see it, I've earned an eye roll or two.

Ms. Ettie finally showed up, and I was happy to let the conversation center around the hero of the hour's Georgetown plans. That sounds more bitter than it should. Simon has a way of leaving you feeling almost jealous, but not quite. I guess because, as Mr. Everything in high school, Simon *was* legitimately exceptional. Yeah, he had a big ego, but he had a bigger heart, and his choosing us—those "skinny, high-yellow, faggot-ass Mathis niggas"—as his best friends made me feel pretty exceptional too.

It was just past nine o'clock by the time Simon and I cruised Antoine's back roads to the highway. His truck still had that new-car smell.

"Man," Simon said, "I forgot how dark these country roads get."

"What're you reading?" I asked.

"Tim O'Brien. Read him?"

"Nah."

"You should. Dude left fucking hand grenade pins on every page."

"Nice." If I ever got my act together and started writing seriously, I'd have to use that line.

Simon gunned onto I-35 toward Oklahoma City.

"So you're writing now?" he asked.

"Yeah. Sort of." I flipped the knob on his air conditioning down, mumbling, "Fucking cold." Then I looked directly at Simon. "Yeah. I'm writing now. Why?"

"Whoa. Calm down, young buck. I'm just asking."

I took a breath.

Simon drummed his thumbs on the steering wheel in time to Outkast and CeeLo's beat.

"In due time."

"In due time," I responded, relaxing into a smile. "Yeah. I'm writing. Trying to anyway." I watched his eyes in the rearview mirror. "Working on a fantasy novel. It's been slow going, to be honest."

"Keep at it."

I began to answer and then noticed our exit approaching.

"Hold up! Hold up!" I said. "Get off here."

"This exit?"

"Yeah, then right on Classen."

"Here?"

"Yep."

"A strip joint?"

"Mmmmm-hmmm."

Simon laughed and pulled into Lil' Darling's parking lot.

"Look who's the coolest grad student in OU's Department of English Lit-er-a-ture," he said, drawing out the last word in a terrible imitation of a posh British accent.

"The competition ain't stiff," I said.

Simon swung into a parking spot a little ways from the entrance.

My boots crunched onto the gravel parking lot. "A friend of mine works here."

Under the riot of stars overhead, the streetlights cast eerie shadows off the trucks' gun racks. In the gloomy glow, a lone figure pissed on the side of the building.

"Classy joint," Simon said.

The man took a long time tucking his junk away, almost like he'd forgotten how. Finally, dude stuffed it through his fly with the care one gives a dirty handkerchief. Then he lurched in our direction.

Soul Patches' booze-creased face brightened at the sight of me, and for half a second I pictured exactly what he must have looked like as a young man. Then something flicked and Soul Patches turned Viking wild, red with rage under the streetlights.

Simon stepped in front of me just as Soul Patches began to shout, "If you're hanging out at this place at your age, where the fuck are you gonna be when you're old as me?"

Then, without waiting for an answer, he staggered past us.

"Your 'friend' who works here?" Simon asked.

We laughed, but only for a couple seconds.

"Dude kind of has a point," I said.

Simon snorted. "Now I really can't wait to see this place."

We wove through the small crowd inside to a table not far from the catwalk. House music bumped from the DJ booth. I saw what Daphne meant about Lil' Darlings on the weekend.

"Hey, Gabs," Alois hollered at me from behind the bar. "Soda water and Crown?"

"Just a splash. For the color." I shouted back, drawing a chuckle from a gaggle of heavyset cowboys at the counter. I jerked a thumb in Simon's direction. "Sam Adams for him."

Simon dabbed a finger on the sticky-with-alcohol table, then wiped it on his jeans.

"My first time here on a Friday." I looked around the bar and thought of all the Dungeons & Dragons campaigns Michael, Simon, and I had started in seedy taverns. "This place can be full of the ghastliest people sometimes."

"A banquet of orcs," Simon said, staring at the catwalk even though no one was dancing yet.

I flipped over a Rolling Rock coaster and patted my pockets for a pen to jot down the phrase. A banquet of orcs. I wasn't sure where this burst of literary motivation was coming from, but I planned to take advantage.

Then that spooky laughter at the beginning of "Feel Good Inc." came on, and I knew my girl was up. I couldn't have timed things better if I'd tried.

Daphne strode onto the catwalk in combat boots, a sports bra, and camouflage shorts, seizing the pole like it owed her money.

Each pivot, pirouette, and pause was electric with emotion. And goddamn, her thighs looked strong. With a groaning flash in her eyes, like she was having a conversation with God, Daphne kicked one of those calves up past her temple. Then she whipped into a spin, releasing the pole as if falling off a cliff before dropping hard into the splits.

She pushed up with a snarl and zeroed in on our table. The room shrank as Daphne stepped off stage in our direction. She froze, letting the hypnotic beat wash over her body, then whipped one of those thick legs onto Simon's shoulder with the kind of toe-to-hip line that dancers kill for. Daphne craned her neck toward Simon, and her expression softened enough to coax him into leaning in, as if expecting a kiss.

Then Daphne's eyes narrowed to slits, and she shoved Simon's forehead, hoisting her leg off his shoulder in a flawless grand battement. And with that, Daphne paced backstage, head high, and without a backward glance.

We burst into applause with the rest.

I'm not sure how many moments of utter happiness you get in life, but this was one of mine. The type of feeling you get three or four times before dying, if you're lucky.

The DJ keyed the mike. "Ladies and gentleman, Deliiii-laaaaaah!"

Simon blew a long, lip-fluttering raspberry. "Your friend?"

"That's her."

"She didn't try for any tips."

"The first dance is for intrigue. The rest are for tips," I said, winking and feeling for an uncomfortable moment like a pimp.

Simon and I brought our hands together in a silent ovation as Daphne sat at our table a few minutes later.

"Simon, this is . . ."

"Daphne," she interrupted. "Delilah's my stage name."

"That was good, Daphne," I said. She knew I didn't throw around the g-word carelessly.

Daphne pointed a fingernail at me, and I thought she would make a joke. Instead she met my eyes and said, "Thanks," like she meant it.

Then Daphne turned to Simon. "You should have seen me before I got a hold of this guy."

"I've been watching this guy dance since we were kids," Simon said. "That reminds me, what's all this about going overseas?"

"The Ukraine thing?" Daphne said.

"Ukraine?" Simon asked. "To dance?"

"No." I looked from Simon to Daphne, spooked by how quickly they'd fallen into familiarity. "To teach English. To write. To get the hell out of Oklahoma."

"Why'd you quit dancing anyway?" Simon asked.

I shrugged. "Teenage angst."

"Something to do with his parents," Daphne addressed Simon as if I were not present. "Mostly his dad."

"Yeah." Simon nodded. "I could see that."

They were wrong. Or at least not completely right. The truth is that convincing yourself to heave, point, leap, fall, and then peel off bloodied, cracked toenails afterward takes an absolute, arrogant, almost religious belief in your ability. A belief I lost at eighteen years old, with my back to one of the mirrored walls in Sergei's studio in Oklahoma City.

"Decent. Not good. Maybe one day . . ." Sergei's voice dwindled into a frown. "But no, Gabriel. I have seen great. You will never be that."

I stared down the rows of dominos I'd stacked just to get to decent and felt equal parts gratitude and hatred for Sergei. Dancing is a commitment that refutes real life. When the thing that had been my crux suddenly wasn't, I'd fallen into a cascade of disappointing my dad's expectations faster than he could lower them.

Daphne and Simon stared at me over their drinks. I couldn't remember the question or who'd asked it, but I'd clearly taken too long to answer.

Simon spoke as if he'd just read my mind. "Frank just wants you to work hard. Lord knows you've done that. We all have." Then he reached across the table and squeezed my shoulder. "You're so full of talent, Gabs. Always have been. You're going to be fine."

I looked at Simon and felt as if my entire life had gathered in my throat. I managed a nod.

Daphne turned to Simon with a look that made me want to give the two of them some privacy. "What about you? Why'd you quit the army?"

"Air force," Simon corrected, then shrugged. "Midtwenties angst."

Daphne returned his grin. "Tell me about it." She intertwined her fingers and rested her chin on top. "What was the most useful thing you learned in the military?"

I sighed with force.

Simon set his eyes on me. "Public service is a good thing, Gabriel. An honorable thing." He'd clearly been waiting for an opportunity to tell me that.

"That's how you think of the military? Public service? Like being a teacher or a . . ." I thought garbageman, but said, "fireman."

"Yep." Simon took a defiant swig of beer. "You know what? I went to war more than once to protect your right to stupid-ass opinions. You've been partying. I've been sitting at FOBs that stunk of bloated groundwater, kerosene, and burning shit."

"Really? *That's* your argument? Well, gee." I brought my middle finger to my eyebrow in a "fuck you" salute. "Thank you for your service. And now the rest of us don't get to say anything about the military except how much we support it? Is that it?"

Simon showed me his middle finger, before speaking to Daphne. "The most useful thing I learned in the military was water confidence."

"Is that an air force way of saying you learned how to swim?" I said.

"No. I knew how to swim. What I learned in the military was confidence in the water." He took a swig of his beer. "Swim qualification at pararescue indoc is fucking medieval, man. Jesus Christ, I fucking hated that pool. Bobbing around with your lungs deflating like bags in a demon's fist. The instructors called passing out in the water 'going to meet the wizard.' I met that motherfucker three times."

Simon had our attention.

"Shit wasn't fair. I'm negative buoyant as a motherfucker. Those hayseed white boys would pop in a pinch of Copenhagen and breeze through the pool work, while I suffered. And that got me to thinking. Nothing's fair. None of it. My family. Yours. Antoine. My dad. School. Football. Wrestling. The military. Nothing's fair. This was the first time in my life I'd ever been really physically challenged. I had to work three, four times harder in the water, and that's just the way it was. We were all just men in the arena. Accepting *that* was my water confidence. That was the answer, buried in all that suffering."

Daphne looked at Simon spellbound, but I wasn't ready to concede.

"That speech sounds practiced, Sy."

Simon smiled, sat back in his chair.

"Do you remember *Elfquest*?" he asked.

I sucked my teeth and gave him a look. Just who the hell did Simon think he was talking to about *Elfquest*? "Man, I was the one who introduced *you* to that comic."

Simon waved off this crucial point. "Take a guy like Cutter, right? If he had been a human he would have been a soldier, a politician, and an artist. But for those elves there was no difference between those professions."

I smirked.

"But it's not like that for humans," Simon continued, "or at least not for the ones here in the States. Here those first two professions are men in a way the last isn't."

Daphne and I waited for Simon to continue, to somehow tie this tortured thread together.

Instead, he raised his beer to his lips.

"So . . . ?" Daphne prompted.

"So." Simon took a breath and knifed four extended fingers across the table in my direction. "So, don't let anyone tell you what it means to be a man, Gabs. Your path isn't mine. Or Frank's."

"Fair enough." I raised my glass. "To men and elves."

Simon clinked his Sam Adams against our drinks. "But show some respect in the meantime, got-dammit."

His Frank impersonation wasn't bad.

After Daphne's shift, we returned to her place to drink. Loudly.

"We have the right," Simon shouted, leaning into the coffee table in front of Daphne's couch. "No! No! The fucking duty! To pick and choose—to cobble together what it means to be a patriot!"

"I'm a patriot to heaven!" I was having a blast. "My loyalties are to truth and justice!"

When Daphne finally set upon Simon, I suspected that it was partly just to get us to shut the fuck up.

She kissed him with animal ferocity. But, while Erykah Badu crooned over the stereo, Simon didn't seem to be kissing her back. Let me tell you something: restraint can be sexy as hell.

Then Daphne clasped my crotch and—yearning to feel close to him and unawed by her—I dove in. To hell with lifeguards.

We focused on Daphne, tore off her clothes and our own, but came up for air in the same moment and saw our eyes reflected in each other's stare. I watched the shadow of Simon's silhouette, lean and powerful, running his hands from Daphne's shoulders to the curve of her back. He never released my gaze.

Simon planted a hand on the small of Daphne's back and pulled my cheek to his. His face was warm, damp. I dropped my forehead onto his trapezius, just below his ear, shuddered there, tasted his sweat. I lifted my face to Simon's and exhaled, blowing a fine mist of sweat off my lips, inches from his mouth.

Simon pushed my chest so gently that it felt like encouragement. Then with a stupid grin he imitated TJ, one of me and Michael's worst tormentors back in Antoine.

"Them faggot-ass Mathis niggers."

Harkening back to those days in Antoine, when, in many ways, our very existence depended on Simon. I used to wonder how someone could not be enthralled by Simon. Michael certainly had been. Simon and I went no further. Not out of fear—that night our hearts had no more room for fear—but because of Michael.

Still, we both breathed easier after that moment. Some barrier lay decimated there, on Daphne's bedspread.

Simon reattached his mouth to Daphne's, while I dropped down to kiss the inside of her thighs.

In the end, she was the one who maestroed the event.

"Jesus Christ, Gabriel!" Daphne reached down, letting her hand sink deep into my Afro before grasping and giving my head a firm shake. "It's a clit, not a speed bag!"

She freed her mouth again to scold us. "Guys! Guys! Do Stevie Wonder impersonations if you can't stop laughing."

We giggled, bit each other's earlobes, and kissed one another's foreheads. Eventually I collapsed onto our empress's shoulder. Simon passed out on her thigh.

The next morning, I woke and sat bolt upright in bed, lips sticky with Laphroaig and Daphne. The sun peeked through the blinds. The apartment bristled with Daphne's singing and the aroma of coffee and bacon.

Simon appeared in the doorway holding two crimson glasses. "Bloody Mary?"

The glass's contents singed my nose hairs.

"Man. You really are decompressing."

"Breakfast of champions." Simon sat on the edge of the bed. "Why'd you quit dancing, Gabs?"

"It stopped feeling worth it." I took a gulp, wiped my lips with the back of my hand, and placed the glass on the nightstand. We'd slept with the same woman last night—had slept with each other too, really—and *now* I feared sounding precious?

"Maybe writing holds as much as the stage. I just need to have the courage to see it. And I can't see it from here." I paused, felt the pleading in my voice. "You know what I mean? I can't see a got-damn thing from here."

Simon laughed, clinked his glass against mine on the nightstand. "Ukraine?"

"Yeah, I guess Ukraine it is. What about you?" I asked. "Six, seven months is a long time to decompress. Are you going to head back to Michael's?"

We listened to Daphne singing along with the hallelujah chorus in the kitchen.

"I think I'm going to stay around here for a bit." Simon stood up. "Come get something to eat."

I took another sip of the Bloody Mary, replaced the glass on the nightstand, and collapsed back onto the pillow. "Sure. One sec."

I stared at the ceiling. The room was becoming too warm.

In the kitchen, Daphne told Simon something.

An edge crept into Simon's response.

Daphne shot back with venom.

Then a moment of silence, broken by both of them laughing.

Insufficiently braced to face them just yet, I closed my eyes and conjured up the image of Daphne on stage—kicking, spinning, powerful—utterly undiminished.

5 | Missionaries, Mercenaries, and Misfits

Mogadishu, Somalia
March 2005

> When God made Somalia, he laughed.
> —African Proverb

THE YAQSHID ANIMAL MARKET is shit, dust, and hair. Piles of decapitated camel heads with lustrous eyelashes and dopey, cartoon lovesick expressions. Baby-faced militiamen with darting, jaundiced eyes. Goats halfheartedly hopping on each other's backs to fuck, then giving up in the compressed heat. Beggars so wracked by polio that they seem to be sitting on piles of brown pick-up sticks with toes. Merchants spitting into each other's faces over how many eggs a jug of camel's milk should fetch. A concentration of chaos only Somalis could achieve. And—Jesus H. Christ—do you love them for it.

In 2005, Yaqshid is the most dangerous district in the most dangerous city on the planet, and the US government—directly and through intermediary companies like the one you work for, Viable Solutions—is flirting with some of the most brutal warlords Mogadishu has ever known. Men like your client: Abdullahi-Deere.

When you think "warlord," you imagine a gold-toothed, bare-chested, ammunition-bandolier-strapped badass perched on a leopard-print throne with scantily clad concubines clinging to his calves. You're disappointed to find that Abdullahi-Deere sports linen leisure suits, a short-cropped salt-and-pepper Afro, and wire-rimmed spectacles. But, measured in terms of being an asshole, Abdullahi-Deere's one of the biggest warlords you've ever met.

You and the two other members of your "mentor team"—Moussa and Ibrahim—meet Abdullahi-Deere in his Yaqshid office at the beginning of the contract in March 2005.

Peeling plaster flaps in the air conditioner's freezing breeze. Despite the bourbon-brown leather sofa and loveseat, Abdullahi-Deere doesn't invite any of you—not even Ibrahim, who's Kenyan Somali—to sit. A polished oak desk that looks like it got lost on the way to a Vermont antique store centers the room. The desktop's clean, save for a shoddy wood carving of the Somali flag stretched between the jaws of two prancing cheetahs. You doubt the day-to-day demands of warlording require much in the way of office environment.

Ibrahim—rail thin with eyebrows so prominent they look hair sprayed—begins the pleasantries in Somali. "This is Simon, our American mission medic."

Behind his desk, Abdullahi-Deere glowers like a schoolyard bully, before responding in English, "He looks Ethiopian."

You are tall, dark skinned, and sharp featured. Ibrahim made the same observation when you met him in Nairobi last week. For Somalis this is not a compliment.

"And young," Abdullahi-Deere adds, with the casual scorn of one unused to disagreement. At twenty-six, you're the youngest expatriate on Viable Solutions' staff. But you have more background than most of the guys on the other mentor teams, so fuck him.

"And this," Ibrahim continues, "is Moussa, our Chechen mission security officer."

"Security officer?" Abdullahi-Deere sucks his teeth.

Moussa bristles. You feel that guilty relief of watching the coach bitch out the other wide receiver. Before meeting your "mission security officer" you assumed Chechens were a swarthy people. But Moussa's ruddy and freckled, thick in the middle, with a receding hairline and dense beard.

"The only reason you two are still alive." Abdullahi-Deere waves a hand around his head, indicating, you suppose, Yaqshid, his district. "Is because." He places his palms on the desk and leans in. "I. Want. It. So."

Hands clasped behind your back, and shivering in the artificial chill, you've never felt so far from home. And that's exactly what you wanted.

⚘

According to your contract with Viable Solutions, four weeks in Mog earns you one week of debauchery in Nairobi. Just enough to keep the stress at a low simmer.

During your conference-call interview—which you did in your draws in your mom's kitchen in Antoine—Moussa and two assholes from the Nairobi office detailed the mechanics of the R&R scheme before breathing a word about the actual job. Then, obviously reading, Moussa recounted, "The role of the mission medic is to build relationships that will strengthen US partners' emergency medical response capacity."

"What does that mean exactly?" you asked.

"Visit hospitals, meet doctors, exchange professional information." Moussa sounded as if he were explaining the fry machine to the new guy at Arby's. "Shit like that." The US-funded contract called for a "mission medic," so Viable Solutions was hiring one.

You do your homework among the expat crowd in Nairobi during your first R&R and find Dr. Omar, a hard-drinking, chain-smoking, French Moroccan emergency physician working in Mogadishu's Banadir Hospital. Contracted through the International Red Crescent Society—one of the few humanitarian agencies still operating in the Somali capital—the altruistic doctor is a welcome change from the Viable Solutions crew.

Three times a week, you assist, advise, and query, but Doc Omar, in melodically accented English, decides. Between patients, he feeds the stray cats in the Banadir compound and tries to convince you to go to medical school. Playing Doc Omar's nurse at Banadir gets you more real trauma experience than your six years as a pararescueman.

The "through and through" injuries, typical of medium-caliber weapons like the AK-47, are easy: plug-and-patch jobs. It's the smaller bullets—the ones that get lodged in the patients—that are a bitch. At least half the weapons-related injuries you treat in Banadir belong to kids under the age of five. At first, the skeletal children's Bambi-eyed silence and glue-caked noses freak you out.

"It gets easier," Doc Omar says, pinky past the first joint deep in his nostril. With his free hand, he tops off your teacup with Bombay Sapphire. You have never met a more unembarrassed nose picker, nor drank more constantly.

"G and T," Doc Omar says. "Best way to fight off the malaria."

You're pretty sure that's not how quinine works.

You learn to ignore the patients' grimaces when tapping around for the *clink-clink* of .38s lodged in thighs and shoulders. But you never shake the stench: a mixture of excrement, sweat, and despair. Or the faces of the mothers, etched with pain and fear but not a hint of indignation—as if Mogadishu has squeezed every drop of human dignity out of their emotions. Wiry and tough, the Somali men remain haughty through interventions that feel less like twenty-first-century emergency medicine and more like Crusader-era torture sessions; this leaves you impressed, until Doc Omar reminds you, "They eat better than the women."

Via email you tell Michael—whose job in New York you scarcely understand—that you're "doing God's work."

His reply, "It sounds more like you're undoing man's."

Swatting flies on the covered veranda in the heavily fortified Peace Hotel—which hosts Viable Solutions' setup along with the Red Crescent's expat staff—you find you can't shut up about the bridges you're building between the company and the humanitarian community. You desperately need your work to matter.

Moussa looks up from a plate of stewed chicken bought live in Yaqshid the day before. He waves a drumstick in your direction and asks, "If vegetarians eat vegetables, what do humanitarians eat?"

Before you can answer, Ibrahim interjects, "Humanitarian work keeps people alive; development work gives them a reason to want to stay that way."

"Yeah. Okay, Ibrahim." You curl your lip. "That shirt and slacks don't change the fact that your job is to beg Abdullahi-Deere for the privilege of installing shitters in his district."

Moussa laughs.

You sneak glances of Ibrahim picking meat off a thigh bone with his creepy wizard fingers. The bruise on Ibrahim's forehead signifies his devotion to Islam in the same way cauliflower ears signify devotion to wrestling.

Ibrahim dabs his fingers clean on a cloth napkin. "I refuse to treat my country like a war zone."

"But it is," you reply.

"Does not mean I have to treat it that way."

A Kenyan medic from one of the other mentor teams clatters a metal plate of chicken onto the wooden table and pulls up a plastic lawn chair.

Your *jambo jinsi wewe* earns a laugh from your fellow paramedic. "Better to say *habari gani*, Simon."

Ibrahim's lips compress into a thin line while you catch up on the curriculum for the first-aid classes for Abdullahi-Deere's men.

The Kenyan medic scarfs down his food, then runs to join his team's convoy in Peace Hotel's courtyard.

"Why do you waste your time with that slave tongue?" Ibrahim asks.

Moussa winks. "Because it helps get you laid in Nairobi."

"My ancestors were slaves," you tell Ibrahim. "Yours fucked camels."

Ibrahim surprises you with a snorting laugh. "Correction: Abdullahi-Deere's ancestors fucked camels. My people are city folks. Mogadishu natives. The Marehan clan. Siad Barre's clan. We'd long run by the time Abdullahi-Deere and these other camel herders started squatting here. At this point, it's as if the clans don't even hate each other anymore, they just kill each other out of habit."

Ibrahim launches into a soliloquy about the brutal long-time dictator whose ouster triggered the country's present perpetual war.

"Somalia needs another Siad Barre. This country cannot be governed, only ruled." Then Ibrahim adds, almost to himself, "The question is if any of these Abdullahi-Deeres are strong enough to do it."

Ibrahim's voice takes on a defensive tone as he gestures around Peace Hotel's ugly, HESCO-fortified interior—the few acres of Mogadishu real estate where you feel semisafe.

"You should have seen Mogadishu under the mighty mouth, Simon. A cosmopolitan, Mediterranean capital. The most beautiful city in Africa."

Moussa smirks and points at Ibrahim. "You ran from your war." He shifts his finger in your direction. "You fought in your wars and returned home." Moussa jams a thumb into his chest. "I was born and raised in war. Just like Abdullahi-Deere's men. I am at home. Here. Now."

He's right. None of you—not even Ibrahim—click with Abdullahi-Deere's militiamen the way Moussa does.

According to the contract, Moussa's role is to "empower US government partners to attain self-sufficient security solutions." Or, more specifically, pleading with Abdullahi-Deere for the privilege of training his militia to shoot straight. Every morning you, Moussa, and Ibrahim line up the militia in Peace Hotel's courtyard to inspect weapons and equipment, all of which—from the blue baseball caps and loadbearing vests to the AK-47s—Viable Solutions has issued. One could accuse the US "War on Terrorism" of many things, but not tight purse strings.

"When was the last time you unloaded this magazine?" Moussa asks the militiamen during one of these inspections, with Ibrahim translating.

Moussa tosses you the offending magazine. You lift it for the three columns of men to see.

"Gentlemen," Moussa continues, "the springs wear out if you don't periodically unload them."

The mostly teenage Somali militiamen snap out palm-forward salutes and flash khat-stained teeth in competition for Moussa's praise.

All the men you respected growing up had been fighters. Your coaches. Frank. Pat, the senior marine EOD tech who took you under his wing at Camp Vance. The father and grandfather you'd never met—one who'd fought for the state, the other an agitator against it—the two strains in your bloodstream, pumping your heart.

That pastor your mom insisted that you speak to in New Orleans was the only person besides your mother who knew both your father and grandfather.

"You can tell the story of white leadership in this country without once mentioning the Federal Bureau of Investigation," he said. Then—looking like an overstuffed suitcase in that Friar Tuck getup—he held your gaze for a split second too long, so you could understand that he had just explained something profound.

But what that fat pastor didn't understand was that you'd never cared about causes. You cared about courage.

As far back as you can remember, joining the military and serving abroad had been central to your idea of legitimacy.

Long before Daphne, before the baby—back when you still had an ethos and the seemingly endless supply of fucks that goes along with it. During your senior year of high school Michael referred to your pending enlistment as "indulging your fascist side." You understand fascism's primal appeal in a way Michael can't. But the Somali militiamen's susceptibility to it—their eyes begging for a leader to worship—frightens you.

All the militiamen chew khat. The trade of the leafy, bitter amphetamine is the only business the war didn't affect. Abdullahi-Deere's men are brutal, drugged up, teenage gun thugs, but they are also *your* brutal, drugged up, teenage gun thugs. The Somalis shoot vigor through everything. From their rough embraces to their discussions that always seem on the verge of fistfights.

Yeah, you like the militiamen. Absolute angels compared to some of the motherfuckers you worked with in Afghanistan—men you sometimes caught staring at you like they were wondering if the top of your head would make a good ashtray. But your rapport with Abdullahi-Deere's men doesn't touch Moussa's. After training sessions with the militiamen, Moussa buzzes around the office with absolute schoolgirl giddiness.

"Wow." You grin at your Chechen colleague. "Look at Mr. Been-There-Done-That bubbling optimism."

"Think you can take this old man, huh?" Moussa feigns a grappling lunge in your direction.

From his stocky frame, you rightly guessed Moussa had once been a wrestler. His ample midsection suggests that while he has long stopped training like a heavyweight contender, he never stopped eating like one.

You pin him easily, but he's trained long enough for the wrestler's backstep and arch to become reflexes.

"Ten years ago I would have given you the run for the money," Moussa says, grinning, hands on his knees.

"I bet." You huff a bit more than necessary for the sake of Moussa's ego.

"You know," Moussa says, "the best grapplers in the world come out of the North Caucasus."

"Nah. Iowa and Brazil. Everyone knows that."

"You want cows, you go to Iowa. You want STD, you go to Brazil. You want grapplers you come to the Caucasus."

You laugh.

Moussa winks. "You want a drink, you meet me on the roof tonight."

On the roof of Peace Hotel, you, Doc Omar, and Moussa pass bottles of Jack Daniels and *samagone*—Russian moonshine, from the aircrew—while emerald and ruby tracer rounds zing across the city.

"The only reason the two of you are still alive is because." You take a breath. It's important to get this bit just right. "I. Want. It. So."

The three of you giggle like teenagers. And Gabs is always saying how terrible you are at impressions.

Moussa touches two fingers to his eyebrow and Doc Omar lazily hoists the bottle.

"To Abdullahi-Deere."

"To Abdullahi-Deere."

"To motherfuckin' Abdullahi-Deere."

There are worse gigs.

"Seventeen days," Moussa tells you.

"Seventeen days," you echo.

From the moment his boots touch Mog, Moussa counts down the four weeks until he can return to his family. His real life is the fifth week, the one with his family in Grozny. For you, neither the drunken seven days in Nairobi nor the pressure-cooker four weeks in Mogadishu are real life. That's the point: Viable Solutions is a haven for vagabonds.

Between slugs of whiskey and teacups brimming with gin, you tell Moussa and Omar that you came to Somalia for the money. Further clarification isn't necessary. Missionaries, mercenaries, and misfits end up in places like Mogadishu. Doc Omar is the first. Moussa is the second. Ibrahim is a hybrid; he's also the only one who pegs you in the third category.

"So you got this Oklahoma prostitute pregnant and ran." Ibrahim doesn't try to mask the disapproval in his voice. Perhaps it was the fact that you didn't drink with Ibrahim that prompted you to open up to him.

"She was a stripper, not a prostitute."

Ibrahim shrugs. You have to admit: it may not be the same job, but it's certainly the same career field.

You were barely in your teens when you embarked on your sexual career. Long before Gabs, who was just a kid, and Michael, who was thoroughly confused back then. Ignoring your idiot fellow athletes in school, you developed an ironclad set of rules. A kind of field manual of sexual conduct. The type of knowledge that didn't serve itself up on a plate. From high-minded fundamentals like Rule Number One, "Never lie." To hard-earned footnotes like "If a girl tells you her name is a flower, a car, or a stone, don't ask what she does for a living." And "If, when you get back to her place, she already has a safe word picked out, just thank your lucky stars and go with it."

With Daphne, you tossed the field manual out the window from the get-go. From that first night when you broke "In MMF three-ways, never touch the other dude." To the biggie, a layer you'd added to Rule Number One way back in high school: "If you're interested only in sleeping with someone, do not, under any circumstances, give the impression otherwise."

You knew better. Yeah, your high school acquaintances were gone. Michael was still in New York, and Gabriel had taken off for Bumfuckistan, Eastern Europe. But this had nothing to do with them. *You* knew better.

You bounced the moment Daphne confirmed that pregnancy, leaving your mom, Frank, Michael, Gabriel—everybody—baffled. But how could you explain the depths of your egomania? How you felt a woman like Daphne didn't deserve a kid from you?

She was supposed to be an interesting segue between the army and Georgetown. Nothing more. Instead, Daphne and her—your—son are the wreck of your goddamned life. Of all the women you dated. Daphne. Funny how that goes. And try as you might, you couldn't help but hate her for transforming you into another absentee black father. What in the world do you say to a child conceived in such circumstances?

Finding a gig abroad wasn't hard. Private military companies were doing everything short of tossing hookers at guys with no-shit special ops experience like you.

You'd been in Mog for three months when your son, Marlon, was born. You'd planned to demand a paternity test. Then your mom emailed you pictures. Marlon is a lighter-skinned version of you. You started sending child support checks. Daphne surprised you by refusing them, so you started an account for the kid.

You keep in touch with Michael and Gabriel. Pat recently reached out via email. You talk to your mother once every couple weeks or so. She doesn't seem mad when you speak, just disappointed. And everyone knows that's worse.

֍

On the afternoon of October 13, 2005, you're far more concerned about diarrhea than your problems back home. Fourteen days into this four-week stint and not a solid shit yet. During your first tour in Afghanistan you self-medicated with an antidiarrheal and managed to constipate yourself for three days. You decided then that, as long as there's water and Ringer's lactate available, it's better to deal with the squirts.

Not daring to fart for fear of the "Somali surprise," you stand with Moussa, Ibrahim, and Abdullahi-Deere outside one of the warlord's compounds in Yaqshid. The location—close to the animal market where Ibrahim wants to start his sanitation project—trumps safety considerations. The two armored SUVs and three technical pickups in your convoy can't all cram into Ibrahim's compound. So Moussa decides to park an SUV and a technical on the street.

A militiaman slouches over the .50 cal in the bed of the technical pickup like a large black spider. Others mill around, twirling their Kalashnikovs like umbrellas. After months of training, you still wince at their weapons handling. Every day you repeat, "There aren't any accidental discharges, only negligent ones." A US military mantra that apparently doesn't translate into Somali well.

Ibrahim's been jumpy all day. His negotiations to drill latrines in this neighborhood have reached the final stage: a face-to-face with the clan elders. Somali society hinges on the clan. Viable Solutions couldn't even park in Yaqshid without the clan elders' permission.

You and Moussa have the luxury of banging out bullshit reports about the militia's progress. *Abdullahi-Deere's men continue to show improvement in their marksmanship skills*— that line you wrote the day one of the boys shot himself in the foot. Seriously. Whereas Ibrahim has to point to actual things—real tangible things like latrines—to prove his worth to the company.

Abdullahi-Deere sneers in response to Moussa's complaints about waiting on the street. "You're perfectly safe anywhere in my district."

It must be exhausting to constantly be this much of a dick.

Ibrahim intervenes. "It's okay. We'll only be about twenty minutes. Less than twenty minutes, right?"

Abdullahi-Deere shrugs.

Moussa sighs. "Try to be quick."

Ibrahim nods.

An hour later, you're still on the street outside the compound, sweat tinged with last night's booze stinging your eyes as your gut squeezes like a dishrag under your Kevlar plate carrier.

Dread of copping a squat in one of the gruesome outhouses you've occasionally been forced to piss in gives way to a final, urgent contraction under your palm. With the checkpoints, it's at least twenty minutes back to Peace Hotel. Even if Ibrahim comes out right now, you aren't going to make it.

You start duckwalking toward the compound.

"Where are you going?" Moussa asks.

"I have to shit, man."

Moussa nods, holds up three fingers to the militiamen, and points at you. Three guys hop off a technical, AKs at the ready.

"Really?" you ask. "To take a shit?"

Moussa takes another drag of his cigarette.

You cinch your sphincter and limp through the gate into the compound. Trailed by the militiamen, you approach the two outhouses in the back. A pair of gnarled, flip-flopped feet poke out from under the wooden door of one. The other outhouse doesn't have a door.

"Nice," you say out loud.

You wrestle off your Kevlar vest, take a deep breath, step into the outhouse, turn around, and drop trou. The militiamen form a protective cordon in front of the outhouse with heartbreakingly sincere military officiousness. You expel everything—bowels, stomach, intestines, liver, lungs, heart, and fucking soul—through your asshole as quickly and forcefully as possible.

One of those fat, almost lethargic, Somali flies lands on your sweat-drenched forehead. You don't dare swat at it, for fear of losing your balance. So you squat—in an eye-watering fog of human feces, with a plump fly perched contentedly on your forehead. A moment so perfectly horrid you can't help but smile.

You don't even consider finding something to wipe with— you roll commando in Mog anyway. You stumble from the outhouse, clenching and unclenching your damp asshole in a sort of systems check, before scooping up your Kevlar vest from the red dirt. You shrug into the plate carrier and take a long, deep breath of fecal-particle-free air. This is how you imagine Catholics feel after confessional.

"Okay, boys," you tell your security detail, certain they don't understand a word, "that's a wrap."

You spot Ibrahim, flanked by militiamen, hugging a stiff-with-formality Abdullahi-Deere near the entrance to the compound. Ibrahim must have hit the right notes during his song and dance at the council of elders.

The sight of Ibrahim grinning under his mad eyebrows as you walk over makes a scratch on your mind. He's not a grinner.

"Ahhh, your Ethiopian medic," Abdullahi-Deere says.

Ibrahim's eyes beg you not to screw up whatever deal he's just brokered.

"I wish," you tell Abdullahi-Deere with a straight face. "There are much better women in Ethiopia than in America."

Abdullahi-Deere clicks his tongue in the back of his throat. "You need a Somali wife, youngster."

You laugh.

Abdullahi-Deere extends his hand to you. Eight months working with the bastard and this is the first time you shake hands. Good thing you didn't wipe.

"No children yet?" Abdullahi-Deere's face doesn't budge, but there's warmth in his voice and something almost like pity in his eyes.

You glance at Ibrahim and then surprise yourself. "One. A son."

"You should have more. What if he dies?" This isn't a threat or an insult, just the advice of a person, a people, a country who take tragedy for granted.

"I'll see you out before your 'security officer'"—Abdullahi-Deere makes quotation marks with his fingers—"has a panic attack."

The militiamen lead the three of you through the gate onto the street. You're still half smiling at Abdullahi-Deere's comment when bits of his head splatter onto your face—some mushy, others spiky and sharp. Understanding takes a moment to catch up. Half of Abdullahi-Deere's head has exploded. Like an overripe jack-o'-lantern—mouth open, teeth broken, cheekbone demolished. A one-in-a-million shot.

The street erupts in a salvo of gunfire that reverberates between your spine and balls as you dash to the armored SUV in front of the compound. The two buildings across the street seem to be dissolving under the militiamen's returned fire. You brace against the armored SUV, coughing in the billowing red dust while dozens of firing pins collide with primers.

Nothing's ricocheting off the vehicle.

"Cease fire! Cease fire!" you shout, waving your hand in front of your face with your palm facing out. A hand-and-arm signal and refrain that you and Moussa have successfully drummed into the militiamen's heads.

The powdered concrete from the pulverized buildings mixes with the spicy aroma of cooked-off ammunition on the suddenly silent street. The whole thing took less than a minute.

You spot Ibrahim grasping his shoulder, hand and shirt blood soaked, eyes wide.

Fuck.

You rip a bandage from your pocket and press it on the wound.

"Hold this on top. Hold it hard," you tell Ibrahim.

Your kit's in the SUV. Still ducking behind the vehicle, you press your fingers under the latch of the rear passenger door. Locked.

Motherfucker.

"Who has the keys?" you yell.

"Here!" One of the Somali drivers bolts from behind the lead technical toward you on all fours, like a bear in a hurry. He slams his back into the driver's side of the SUV and unlocks it, prompting the other doors to click open.

Still crouching, you heave open the armored door, then climb over the car seats and grab your kit.

"Pack him up!" Moussa yells. "We're moving!"

"Come on, get him in here, guys." Keep your voice steady.

You, the driver, Ibrahim, and Moussa pile into the vehicle in a heap of panting dust.

The driver turns the ignition. The VHF radio squawks to life. "Mobile Two, this is Mobile One."

The driver keys the handheld. "Yeah, yeah. Go ahead."

"Tell him we're moving," you say. "Banadir Hospital."

Ibrahim breathes in rasps. *Huh-ah. Huh-ah. Huh-ah.* He mumbles something in Somali.

You rip open your kit. "Lemme get some A/C back here."

The SUV lurches down the dirt road. The lead technical pops off a couple rounds. The A/C sputters to lukewarm life, drying the sweat on your face. Every pothole bounces dressings and scissors out of reach.

Inhale. Hold it. Exhale. Focus past the gunfire, the moon-scaped road, the radio chatter, your fear. Turn down the volume on all of it. Freeze all the shifting phantasmagoria of life and enter a bubble with Ibrahim and Moussa. Just the three of you and one objective: Ibrahim's survival.

Moussa presses the bandage to Ibrahim's wound. You scissor off Ibrahim's shirt.

Left shoulder. Nothing on the chest or abdomen. Exit wound near the clavicle. One of your own militiamen shot him in the back.

Moussa's hands are black from trying to mash Ibrahim back together.

You hand him a fresh bandage. "Press harder."

Moussa nods.

Ibrahim breaks into a spate of gurgling coughs.

You rip open a package of QuikClot and direct Moussa to remove the bandage from the wound. "Okay. Watch out."

The QuikClot granules sizzle to a bright pink on the wound site.

You hand Moussa a third bandage. "Hold this on top. Hard."

Puncture an intravenous giving set through the gold seal on a 500 mL bottle of Ringer's lactate. Run fluid through the line, check for bubbles, then roll up the brake. Pop the top off an orange fourteen-gauge catheter and mop an alcohol swab over Ibrahim's vein. Good stick on the first go. Pinch the vein, withdraw the needle, screw the giving set onto the catheter. Wait for a drip in the chamber, then roll down the brake. Don't push fluids yet, just ensure access.

Ibrahim stares without focus, the way a blind person can look straight at you and not see a thing.

"How you doing, Ibrahim?" you ask. Where the hell is that thermal blanket?

"Hurts," Ibrahim answers.

"Shhh . . . It's okay. Shhhh . . . Just breathe." The same thing you said the last time you let a friend die. Wesley. Wes loved to walk on his hands naked. You'd be in the ready room cleaning your weapon and see this cock, bouncing on a bed of thick, black belly hair past the window to the hallway, like some horrible sea creature. Wes died in your arms, like in a war movie, except with no fade-out to mask the smell of shit seeping from the gaping wound in his gut. His last breaths sounded like he was slurping through a straw.

"There," you say out loud as you find the little gold square of wrapping foil in a plastic bag. You shove it at Moussa. "Open this up."

You're worried about Ibrahim's BP dropping but give him a shot of morphine sulphate through the IV catheter anyway.

Moussa unfolds the crinkling, aluminum foil "blanket." Help him wrap it around Ibrahim.

"It hurts, Simon." Ibrahim's voice is flat, insistent. He's on the cusp of real pain, the kind that reduces humans to screaming animals.

"Can't you give him something?" Moussa demands.

"I did," you snap. "You'll feel it in a second, Ibrahim."

Pop the top on the compressed oxygen. Slip the rebreather mask on Ibrahim's face.

Moussa hands you his mobile. "Talk to Doc Omar."

You inject every bit of calm you can muster into your voice.

"Come," Dr. Omar answers. "We are waiting for you." If the earth cracked open in front of Banadir Hospital and Cerberus leapt out dripping lava from his lips, Doc Omar would tilt his head slightly to the right and light another cigarette.

Amazingly, the bandanaed Somalis wave your convoy right through the big checkpoint at Kilometer 4.

Dr. Omar and several members of his team—all in goggles and scrubs—meet your convoy in the courtyard. Doc opens up the door of the SUV and his people whisk Ibrahim away in a steel scoop stretcher. You rush into the hospital beside them.

Sparrows chase each other between the partially exposed hallway's high glassless windows.

You and Doc Omar exchange rapid-fire sentences.

"I didn't get his BP."

"Did you run any fluid through the IV?"

"I didn't want him to start bleeding again."

"Five milligrams of morphine?"

Dr. Omar stops in the doorway to the ammonia-scented operating theater, grabs your chin, and stares in your eyes.

"What?" You shake free from his grip. "I'm fine, Doc."

"Okay, Simon. Go have a cigarette, then get cleaned up and give me a hand."

"I don't smoke."

"Well go sit down for a minute. And tell Nairobi that Ibrahim is going to need to be MEDEVACed. Of that much I am sure." Doc Omar turns and walks into the theater.

Deflated, you trudge back to the courtyard.

Moussa directs the militiamen where to park the technicals, while shouting into his mobile phone.

You close your eyes. Just for a moment. Just to pull it all the fuck together.

You jump when Moussa places his hand on your shoulder.

"Sorry. So?"

"Doc Omar kicked me out. Told me to catch my breath."

"Not a bad idea."

You look at Moussa.

"You should wash up," he says.

Blood is wedged under your fingernails like poison.

"There's a sink in the . . ." Moussa begins.

"I know where it is."

You get your hands as clean as you can and dry them on your trousers. Then you squat with your back to the hospital wall.

Moussa walks over and hands you the Thuraya. "Nairobi. You're on speaker phone."

"How you doing, kid?" You imagine three empty suits huddled around a landline in the Nairobi office.

"Not bad." You take a breath. "Ibrahim's going to need to be MEDEVACed. We started arranging anything yet?"

Long pause. "Yeah, I don't know if we're going to be able to do that." Another pause. Muffled conversations in the background. A different voice asks, "It's just a shoulder wound, right?"

You drop your gaze to the ground and exhale hard, waiting for the bosses to say something else. They don't. A kitten cute enough for a Hallmark card laps at a puddle of blood near where you unloaded Ibrahim. Your stomach seizes.

"Who the fuck do you guys think you are?" Your voice cracks. "He's going to die. Do you pricks fucking understand that!" Hot sudden tears stream down your face.

"We'll call you back." The line goes dead.

You wipe snot onto the back of your hand, inhale the medicinal smell of hospital soap, and shove the phone in Moussa's direction.

"They're going to call back," you say, as if Moussa has not just heard the conversation.

Moussa nods.

The two of you squat in the dirt with your backs to the hospital. The sun sets the sky ablaze in crimson and pillowed aqua. Dusk doesn't last long this close to the equator. It'll be dark soon.

Moussa lights a cigarette.

"Gimme one of those."

He hands you his cigarette and lights another.

"The only reason the two of you are alive is because." You blow smoke through your nose. "I. Want. It. So."

Moussa snorts, and the ember at the end of his cigarette wobbles. It's not one of your better renditions.

"They're going to let Ibrahim die," you say, kneading your midsection like dough.

"You Americans," Moussa begins, then the sat phone buzzes to life. "Nairobi."

A jolt in your stomach doubles you over.

One of Dr. Omar's assistants comes outside—a new guy, very dark skinned with a spackle of painful-looking razor bumps splayed across his chin and neck. "Simon, Dr. Omar needs you."

You hold up a finger to the assistant and reach for Moussa's phone.

"You didn't say Abdullahi-Deere was dead!" the voice shouts. "Did you try to do something to save *him*? Jesus fucking Christ . . ."

You remove the phone from your ear and look at it. You push the red "end call" button, toss it back to Moussa, and turn to Doc Omar's assistant.

"Tell Doc I'll be right in." First you need to shit.

When Wes died you'd been under fire. Grieving came later, after you'd felt thankful—infinitely thankful—for your own life. When Ibrahim dies—on a steel operating table in a fetid Mogadishu hospital, gurgling crimson-tinged vomit past the plastic tube shoved down his trachea, the evening air thick with humidity and flies—there's nothing to be thankful about.

You peel off blood-caked latex gloves and look up at Doc Omar. His gloves are already off.

Doc Omar digs a finger in his nose and then delicately removes a long, stringy booger from one nostril. He wraps the booger up in a tissue, notices you staring, and then points to the bottle of Blue Sapphire next to the sink.

"It gets easier."

6 | Revolutions of All Colors

Part One

Kyiv, Ukraine
September 2004

Tamara

Papa gave me two pieces of dating advice before he died.

The first, when the subject of introducing him to one of my teenage boyfriends came up.

"Now think hard, Tamarachka." Half of Giga's single, uninterrupted eyebrow furrowed into a caterpillar wink. "Do I *really* need to meet this person?"

The second, years later (and far drunker), after I began traveling internationally for work.

"If you do end up marrying a foreigner, at least marry a black one." Giga flashed burgundy-tinged teeth. "That way I won't have to keep explaining to people why he doesn't speak Russian."

During Soviet times, Papa worked at the Ministry of Agriculture. I'm not sure what his official title had been, but from a very early age I understood that he was a *baryga*—a profiteer. Giga hawked sturgeon from Dushanbe and redirected bananas from Kinshasa in order to tilt the old "to each according to his need" bit in our family's favor.

He infected me with his love of all things American—books, TV, films—and spoke of the folly of our grandfathers and great-grandfathers that had trapped his business genius in "the most stifling environment for innovation ever devised by man."

With his elbow nudging a jug of Alazani wine at our kitchen table, my father taught me the fine art of how to give a bribe and the far darker art of how to take one.

"The Soviet Union only produces three things worth exporting. Weapons, vodka, and political exiles." And this advice also I took to heart; it's partly why I chose my profession and became so good at it.

At that same kitchen table, I watched my father listen to the 1979 Radio Moscow broadcast of Angela Davis receiving the Lenin Peace Prize, his expression equal parts pity and awe.

"The American Negro," he said, as if the combination of their nationality and ethnicity was the most pitiable aspect of their condition. "A people with no counterparts, nor predecessors. A race born of capitalism."

I was twelve years old and imagined a group of people being born out of my economics textbook, marching right off the pages. I'd seen on TV how much those people enjoyed marching.

These were the things I was thinking of when my boss's son dragged me into his English teacher's classroom.

Gabriel

If I could have scripted meeting Tamara, it would have been someplace neutral. Any city would have been a handicap, but drop us in, say, Tokyo. Or Berlin. Completely different scene, right? That's all I'm saying.

Hold up. Scratch Berlin. Tamara speaks German.

Our unscripted meeting occurred during last period on a Thursday, with my Doc Martens kicked up on my desk, under the floor lamp next to my brand-spanking-new leather office chair. I had *The Things They Carried* cracked open over my thighs.

I'd layered clichés on top of half-truths in my fantasy novel's massive Tolkienesque battle scene and was now devouring every bit of war fiction I could get my hands on. Simon's suggestion had been the best yet for the type of details I needed: prying ticks off your ball sack, the smell of human and animal shit, lives lived without the civilizing presence of women, actual fear. I'd left Oklahoma to write and had made the mistake of announcing my ambition to people who would hold me to account. I needed to finish this novel and it needed to be good.

My classroom door yawned open, and the clinically severe hallway lights parted the shadows on the cream-tiled floor.

I heard Sasha Colstinichkin's voice but didn't look up immediately.

"This is him, Tamara. This is Gabriel."

Don't get me wrong. Sasha Colstinichkin was one of my favorite students before I met Tamara. He was definitely my favorite Sasha. (The name is the diminutive of both Alexander and Alexandra, so I had more than a dozen spread over my six classes.) But this was my free block, which meant that I was done teaching for the day. I was just waiting for Max to finish up in the neighboring classroom so we could engage in what had become our traditional pre-bar smoke session.

And then, of course, there was the other thing. Of the eight expat English teachers the Bladoonsky Preparatory Institute recruited that summer, I was the only black dude. Being presented to parents, siblings, and nannies like some sort of mocha-colored unicorn gets old quickly.

I finished the paragraph I was on, glanced over the top of the paperback, and *bam!* Tamara's beauty—a cross between boss lady–business exec and nose-ringed Snow Valkyrie—struck me like a bullet in the brain.

I kicked over my wire mesh trash can scrambling to my feet.

Tamara's eyeballs clicked cyborg-style from the trash can pirouetting a spinning top of shadows under the floor lamp, up to the framed pictures of James Baldwin and Anna Akhmatova on the wall behind me.

"Hey, Sasha." I pointed at the switch near the door. "Get the lights for me, buddy." I turned to Tamara, tapping the novel against my chest. "Yeah, I'm Gabriel. Hi." I tucked the book into my armpit, extended my hand, and blurted, "You're not a nanny." Jesus. Smooth as sandpaper.

The overhead lights flittered to life as she shook my hand. Friendly enough, but not exactly smiling.

I hadn't danced for months by then, not since arriving in Kyiv in July. But all those years in the studio had left me hyperaware of how to hold my body to its best advantage. I used every trick in the book: chin lowered, chest open, hips over knees over toes.

"At long last." Tamara raised a sculpted eyebrow. "Mr. Gabriel."

Everything about her—the sharp, short honey-colored hair, the silver loop adorning her right nostril, the striped slacks that reminded me of something from Ms. Ettie's wardrobe of badass chic—seemed inhumanly precise.

"No, I'm not the nanny. I work for Sasha's dad, but I'm close to the family, so I pick the little guy up from time to time."

Tamara tousled Sasha's mop of unruly curls, and the eleven-year-old took it without complaint. Fucking remarkable.

Tamara jutted her chin at the pictures behind me. "Akhmatova I know. Who's the other?"

"That's James Baldwin." I gave Tamara my version of a starry-eyed artist's shrug. "Two of my favorite writers. I love imagining the conversations those two would have had."

"Akhmatova wrote in Russian. Do you speak?"

Hmmm. More challenge than question.

Before I could respond, Sasha—grinning up at us, utterly forgotten—leapt to my defense. "Tamara! I told you, Gabriel's A-meri-can. He speaks English." That kid was all teeth. Even his teeth seemed to have teeth. I'd heard a couple of my nastier students calling him *cheluyha*—jaws—in the hallways.

I rolled out my most polished Russian phrase, *r*'s stiff as a board. "Well I do speak some Russian, but with a terrible accent."

Tamara nodded, unimpressed. I was seriously studying Russian and, like most Americans, I counted on the world being unceasingly charmed by even my slightest effort outside English.

She continued in Russian, "And Ukrainian?"

Figuring it was best to stop with the Russian while I was ahead, I switched back to English. "You know, lots of people say Ukrainian isn't really a language, just a dialect of Russian."

Tamara sized me up.

"There is," she began slowly, "an anecdote that asks whom Ukrainians should shoot first if we ever again find ourselves beset by both the Germans and the Russians."

Holding her gaze was like trying to stare at the sun.

"Okay. I'll bite," I said, and we both laughed. It felt right, us laughing together. "Who?"

"Whom," Tamara corrected, winking and sprinkling a dash of posh on her accent.

My writer's ego flared heat across my face. Then I smiled. This pomposity was her. I appreciated the glimpse.

"And the answer is we shoot the Germans first. Business before pleasure."

Switching back to Russian, Tamara told Sasha something about horses and being late.

Sasha extended his pale knuckles to me and we bumped fists. Our second fist bump of the day. He'd earned the first for explaining the difference between "I smoked" and "I was smoking" in class.

Sasha was prime bullying material: too thin, too smart (and no good at hiding it), and with rows upon rows of teeth waging an apparently successful campaign against those damn braces. I caught snippets of the cruelty in the hallways, watched Sasha trudge to class early and stay late, and remembered just how shitty being an eleven-year-old can be. The fist bumps, nods, and winks were all accompanied by telepathic messages: "Hang in there, bruh."

Tamara walked out with little Sasha in tow. Shining with her stride—all clacking heels and business slacks hugging the sort of thickness I'd only recently remembered how much I loved.

One baaaaaaad bitch.

Tamara

That was when I decided, watching him with Sasha.

A fling. Nothing serious. He looked very young. Early twenties. At least a decade younger than me.

I hoped he wouldn't say anything too stupid and ruin it.

Gabriel

After Max finished with his class, we smoked in the alley behind Bladoonsky, leaning against the building's exposed brick wall and watching a feral calico dig through one of the dumpsters for lunchroom refuse.

"Her name's Tamara." I handed the joint back to Max, savoring the feel of her name on my lips, and then repeated it in a mutter as if she were a saint. "Tamara."

The dank smell of very strong weed overpowered that of the trash.

"Yeah, I heard you the first time," Max said, raising eyebrows that, despite regular tweezings, remained hell-bent on meeting in the center of his brow.

Max—a Jewish "repatriate" returned to Ukraine from Israel to help care for his ailing father—is the hairiest human being I have ever met. Besides the unibrow, he fully owned it. He left his top three buttons unfastened to advertise the gold Star of David nestled on his woolly chest and claimed that his lumberjack chops were scented with "vermouth and the blood of my enemies." Max is the type of guy who can get away with saying shit like that with a straight face.

Max had been back in Kyiv since completing his service with the Israeli army last year. I met him during faculty orientation in September. Halfway through our first conversation—apropos of nothing, we'd been talking about comic books, for Christ's sake—Max pressed a finger into my chest and said, "Good God, man. Wait until these Cossack bastards get a load of you." He spoke as if my very existence would teach those Cossack bastards a lesson or two. Then he laughed—really laughed—and I understood that, for better or worse, we'd just become friends.

In the alley, Max held the cannabis smoke so long I began to worry that he'd forgotten about the exhaling part. Like I said, it was strong weed.

Max drank and smoked like a writer. Trying to keep up had precluded me from going to bed fully sober for the last three months. Occasionally, I worried that living life like a rock star's Friday night was squeezing writing into the margins of my life. But then I'd read another account of Kerouac stumbling out of the White Horse Tavern or of Cheever watching two hookers play hopscotch with a hotel room key. Steinbeck had learned to take his hangovers as "consequence, not punishment," and so—damn it—would I.

"Your little Sasha's dad is big time in the arms trade," Max said breathlessly, wagging a finger. "Andreyi Colstinichkin. Used to be some kind of director in the Ministry of Defense." He blew smoke in the direction of the cat, who plunged into the depths of the dumpster. "Sasha's babysitter probably makes more than both of us put together."

He paused, considered me for a second.

"If you had one hair on your sack you'd already have her number."

"Fuck you. And she isn't a babysitter. That girl carried herself like she ran Sasha's daddy's business."

"You really like this one. That was quick." Max shook his head. "I worry about you, young man."

"What can I say?" I put on my best Will, Denzel, and Samuel L. mash-up (I'd already discovered how much non-Americans lap up that shtick). "It don't take a whole day to recognize sunshine."

"Not bad."

"One of my dad's lines."

"I'm stealing it."

There are three types of English teachers in the world: those who fancy themselves writers, those who don't fancy themselves writers yet, and those who no longer fancy themselves writers. Max and I are in the first group. For Max this means writing five hundred words a day. After monumental nights on the piss, I'd crack my eyelids from Max's couch to him getting in his five hundred words. His day didn't begin until after those five hundred words. The only thing I'm that consistent with is masturbation.

We got smashed that night. Inspired and highly caffeinated, I spent the next morning locked in my apartment, furiously writing Tamara into my nascent fantasy novel. My goddess of war.

I got Tamara's number from Sasha at school the next week. We began exchanging text messages under the pretext of progress reports on young Sasha's English. I finagled a witty little back-and-forth about the vital distinctions between dwarves, elves, and gnomes into an eventual invitation to meet her and some friends at Cowboys, a pub downtown.

Max and I arrived early and stoned.

The doorman at Cowboys—sports-coat buttons clawing for dear life against his bulk—gave us an evil henchman's grin that was meant well. "Max. Gabreel."

"What's up . . ." Igor? Oleg? Alex? The Orthodox faith's dearth of names gave a guess about a 20 percent chance of accuracy. "Sergei . . . ?"

I almost collapsed under Sergei's palm to my back.

Shto ne rosha, to serosha. Every other mug is a Sergei. In a matter of months, I've jumped from having one Sergei in my life to half a dozen.

Cowboys had all the trappings of a conventional American tourist bar: a Route 66 sign, framed photographs of the filming of one of the *Die Hard* films signed by Bruce Willis, and advertisements for all the shit beers I'd been so happy to escape. The sort of Americana that Tamara claimed to find funny.

The toilet in Cowboys—with its factory-style linoleum walls and that weird, incessant squeaking—was where the tourist facade truly cracked. No urinals or stalls, just a dingy open row of shitters that gave a put-upon sigh when you pulled the dangling torture-room chain to flush. As if halfway through creating this tourist-themed monstrosity, the designers threw their hands up. "Fuck it. Who do we think we're kidding?"

Tamara arrived at the tip of a phalanx of slightly lesser demigoddesses—women who looked like they owned, taught, and ran things.

"Hey, Tamara."

"Hi, Gabriel," Tamara responded, with a half-crescent smile that cascaded through her line of backup dancers. She had probably used me as an excuse to drag them to this odd little museum of American bric-a-brac. I decided to be okay with that; whatever got her here.

"This is Olga," Tamara began. "She teaches at the Kyiv Meteorological . . ."

"So," Max interrupted Olga's CV, "the famous Tamara." He executed about one-eighteenth of a bow.

In a conversational silence just hostile enough to be felt, Tamara regarded Max and then said something to her friends in Russian that I didn't catch through the noise of the bar. The five ladies dispersed to the bar to get drinks. Tamara pushed up to the ledge of the counter next to me.

She ordered a whiskey with ice.

Then Tamara turned from the bartender back to Max with a look of exhaustion. A look that seemed to sigh, "Do you have any idea how many douchebags I've handled today before you?"

"So," Tamara said. "If he's the black Fitzgerald, I guess that makes you the Jewish Hemingway, right?"

Max sniffed. "Nah, this kid's the black Carver and that'd make me the Jewish Cheever."

"Tam," I interjected, "this is Max. His head's up his ass, but his heart's in the right place."

That got a chuckle out of both. I took the opportunity to pick up Tamara and my drinks and escort her away from the bar to a table.

"Where'd you get that line?" Max asked.

"My dad," I said over my shoulder, hand on the small of Tamara's back, guiding her through the expats and Ukrainians united on Cowboys' tiny dance floor—a singular mass of white people gyrating badly.

"I gotta meet that guy." Max's voice faded into the low-fi Ukrainian reggae band pumping through Cowboys' speakers.

Tamara

I shook Gabriel's hand off my back and smiled up at him—a splinter of slender grace embedded on the bar's crowded floor. Between text messages concerned with everyone from Tolkien to Tolstoy, Gabriel had mentioned that he grew up dancing, which explained his posture. Not stiff, but deliberate, like he knew his place in this world.

On my tiptoes, I leaned into his ear and relieved him of my drink. "Let's go for a cigarette."

Holding the tumbler above my head, I nudged through the crowd to the door, confident that Gabriel would puppy-dog behind me to the stairs outside.

I dug cigarettes out of my new Hermès bag and watched Gabriel's eyes widen, as if unsure where to focus. Cowboys lay on the stretch of bars and cafés between Bessarabska and European Squares on Khreshatyk—a boulevard dotted with baroque park benches and streetlights, where the Soviet-era TSUM department store now blinked with screens advertising Benneton and Bvlgari. One of my favorite streets on the planet, with all those steepled, sumptuous apartment blocks, built for the Soviet elite—Red Army generals, commissars, internationally regarded professors—but now inhabited by businessmen like my boss.

Even during the darkest days of the absurd tracksuit banditry of Ukraine's early independence, Khreshatyk remained bright. A candlepower reminder of who we'd always been—from White Russians to Red, from Bolsheviks to perestroika, from bandits to New Russians, to something uniquely Ukrainian, something uniquely ours.

"Time sleeping in this city is time wasted," Gabriel said, in passable Russian.

During our text exchanges he'd mentioned his Russian tutor, Nina. A woman in her early sixties who'd apparently earned a PhD in philology at my alma mater, Taras Shevchenko University. A full professor who tutored Gabriel for pennies on the dollar. A woman from my mother's generation. The generation that remembered Gagarin. The generation whose parents held Stalingrad. The last generation of Ukrainians who'd seen Moscow as the center of the universe, with Kyiv in close orbit. Nina had made the mistake of swallowing the lie that everyone around her was gobbling up. Everyone except people like my father, and what did he get for his trouble? A liver riddled with cirrhosis followed by an early death. Because a normal person understands that it's pointless and dangerous to oppose universal insanity, and rational to participate in it. And no matter what Gabriel said—and he did often say many of the right things—he would never fully "get" what someone like Nina meant to someone like me.

"Agreed," I said in English, tapping a fag out of my box of Gauloises. "Another line from your dad?"

"Suddenly no one thinks I can come up with my own material." Gabriel laughed, brought flame to the cigarette dangling from my lips, and snapped his Zippo shut with a surprisingly impressive martial swipe.

I examined Gabriel like an apple at the market; a man who didn't take himself too seriously couldn't be all bad.

"No," he continued, "that line's definitely not from my dad. He never lived in a city. Well, I guess he might have spent some time in Saigon."

"You mean Ho Chi Minh city. Beautiful place."

My mobile rang in my bag. I held the leather purse up for Gabriel's inspection.

He shook his head, smiled. "Snob."

I took a couple quick puffs, then ground out the cigarette on the heel of my boot. On the phone I answered questions and issued instructions in short bursts of Russian.

"Tyre. Yes. In Lebanon."

Pause.

"Uh-huh." Quick glance at Gabriel. "Yes. And the Khat-tabkas. Mmmm-hmmm."

Pause.

"Okay. Call when it's done."

I clicked the red end-call button and turned to find Gabriel hugging himself in the glow of a knockoff eighteenth-century streetlight, like some black aristocrat poorly cast as an underprivileged orphan.

"Where's your jacket, pumpkin?"

"With Max. In the bar." Gabriel jerked his head toward the sounds of men and women speaking too loudly and drinking too much. "What—what exactly do you do, Tamara? I know what Khattabkas are."

Slang for grenades. Homemade ones actually; the thug on the other end of the line was probably still trying to figure out why I'd called our manufactured ones that.

"Nina taught you that?" I asked.

"No," Gabriel untucked his hands and blew on his fingers. "Max."

"Of course."

"So . . . what is it that you do for a living?"

I tipped the tumbler until the ice clinked my teeth and scrutinized Gabriel for the third time that night. Sweet Sasha's favorite teacher. A liquid-eyed Oklahoma boy on his first jaunt abroad.

I buried my British-accented English under my best Blanche DuBois impersonation.

"Why, honey, I run guns."

I patted his cheek with one hand and extended the tumbler toward him with the other, jingling the ice.

"Now be a dear and freshen this up."

Gabriel

During the next few weeks we knelt next to the menorah memorial in Babi Yar park (Max's grunt when I told him was as close as he ever got to approving of anything Tamara-related), visited Bulgakov's home on Andreevsky Spusk, and gazed up at countless valiant monuments of 'roided-up Slavs unfurling hammer and sickle banners in grim defiance of the people who continued to build the world's best engines.

Tamara's mother was Russian. Her father—that blessed soul who'd indoctrinated his daughter in everything from *Hawaii Five-o* to Paul Robeson—hailed from Georgia ("Tbilisi, not Atlanta"). Her parents met and married in Kyiv and spoke Russian at home. Tamara's "mongrel" (her word, not mine) ethnicity made her an unlikely patriot.

About her job. Sasha's dad owned a multinational shipping company, so it wasn't as if Tamara transported only weapons. Mostly weapons, maybe. But not just weapons. During the next few weeks of flirtatious sexless limbo, Tamara tried to explain the difference between white, black, and gray arms sales. While she spoke, I imagined Makhachkala militants passing a block of plastic explosives around a coffee table and half-naked kids mowed down in a Sudanese desert.

Before Tamara, I'd never appreciated the artificiality—the pure fiction—of borders. She called them "lines men drew on maps" and discussed mountains ranges, oceans, roads, weather, and sometimes even troops and security forces, but never borders. Like some global dermatologist, her job was to spot pores in countries' borders.

I don't remember if I stopped asking for explanations before she stopped offering them, but our silent resolution not to discuss her work in detail was a relief for both of us.

Golden Gate Bar became our go-to spot. After a couple nights of Tamara picking up the tab, I made a move for the leather billfold lying between our empty glasses on the table.

Laughing, Tamara counterfeinted her hand around the check like a boxer.

"Come on, Gabs. It doesn't really matter, does it?"

"Let me get this one."

"Sure." She scrunched her nose as if smelling sour milk, and the silver loop in her nostril jiggled. "Whatever. In that case, let's have another."

That night, Tamara told me that her father and boss had served together in the Soviet Army in Afghanistan. My dad served in Vietnam. Both conflicts that those with means avoided. Something about this felt like working-class solidarity, and I loved it. Thinking of my father, I rattled off a couple lines of Wordsworth I'd stumbled across in my war reading.

> Who is the happy Warrior? Who is he
> That every man in arms should wish to be?
> . . . .
> As more exposed to suffering and distress;
> Thence, also, more alive to tenderness.

Tamara reached across the table, placed a hand on my cheek. "Is that the war you're writing into your novel? A pretty good time if you can just survive it?"

Yes. I'd ignored the war stories that had surrounded me all my life and was writing fantasies, and not the good kind either.

I groped for the words to answer Tamara. I was pretty drunk.

"War is not just combat, Gabriel. Its main protagonists aren't just soldiers, whom you seem to think of as only male."

Her hand dropped from my face to my chest and for a long while she didn't speak. Her face could have been cut from marble—terrifying, excruciatingly beautiful.

"Akhmatova called war a time when only the dead smile, happy in their peace."

My heart pounded against her fingers.

"That's war," Tamara said. "Write that."

I leaned across the table. Instead of meeting me, she clenched a fistful of my T-shirt. Then flattened her palm against my chest and shoved me back into my seat.

"Okay, youngster. How about one last round?"

Like I said, one baaaaaaaaaad bitch.

Tamara

I sent him home alone again that night.

I woke the next morning in my long red, white, and blue "Liberia!" T-shirt, panties balled up in the corner of my bedroom where I'd tossed them before collapsing onto the Egyptian cotton. I dragged myself to the toilet, splashed my face, and then patted it dry, recalling what Gabriel had said last night just before I put him in a cab—young, drunk, and happy.

"You're a Valkyrie. A goddess of war."

The face in the mirror twisted into a snarl. With my nose ring and mess of blonde hair pulled up into a hornet's nest, it was not hard to envisage my reflection scouring frozen steppes, spear in hand, eyes squinting in the sun. I loved the way Gabriel saw the world, the way he saw me.

I trudged into the kitchen. The blue on the refrigerator blinked 10:04 a.m. Close enough. I poured three fingers of whiskey into a glass, took the ice tray out of the freezer, cracked it, and dropped two cubes into the amber liquid. A sip shot steel through my spine. I picked up my mobile from the counter.

Did you eat yet today?

I wished I'd slept with him already, before all this.

Gabriel

I banged out a response immediately. *In the middle of a passage! Gotta finish . . .*

My phone vibrated with her response.

The great American fantasy novel can wait 30 minutes. Eat.

I imagined Tamara's eyes rolling to somewhere near the top of her skull. I needed to step it up.

I thumbed my Nokia as if racing to unlock the nuclear code that would save humanity.

I need inspiration. My characters are stuck. Help me, Tam! You're my only hope!

The *Star Wars* reference might have gotten at least a smirk.

My phone whirred with her challenge.

You couldn't handle me as your Akhmatova.

I fired off: *If you were music, I would listen to you ceaselessly and my low spirits would brighten.* I waited five seconds, then followed up with: *You will hear thunder and remember me, and think: he wanted storms.* That was all the Akhmatova I had on tap.

A minute. Two. I ran my hand through my 'fro and tripled down. *Tell me to get there and I'm there. You know that. You've known that from the moment we met.*

I tossed the phone on the couch and strode into my kitchenette in a pair of raggedy striped draws, feeling like a man.

I cracked open a beer and leaned against the countertop. My phone buzzed just as I tipped the bottle to the ceiling. I tore my way back to the couch.

Get here.

We wrestled off each other's clothes and left them balled at her front door. When our bodies finally met—bodies that history, geography, and circumstance should have kept apart—it felt like our ancestors were cheering us on.

Afterward, she looked up at me from my still-thudding chest.

"Are you sure you can handle storms?"

Tamara

"Definitely a Cat. II," Gabriel paused, gave me a lopsided grin. "Maybe a weak Cat. III."

Which is to say he never really answered that question.

But *chert poberi* could he make me laugh. He gave me stomachaches from tales of his brother and friend in a small-town Oklahoma reminiscent of any Ukrainian backwater. Stories downright Soviet in their lack of privilege. And yet, here he was. In another country in his twenties, teaching, writing. A go-getter, desperately—and in my mind inexplicably—trying to pass himself off as a waster.

I rolled onto my back on my bed, clasped his hand to my leg.

One had to have a heart of stone to hear the story Gabe had just told—of a boy he'd seen killed—and not laugh. Unlike most Americans, Gabe seemed to understand just how much of this world's tragedy so richly deserves laughter.

"Why don't you write *these* stories?" I asked.

He looked at me, astounded. Giga used to say that a strange new light can be just as frightening as the dark.

I dug his fingers into my thigh until it hurt. "You are allowed to write those stories too, you know?"

The weeks eased into a month. Two. I watched Gabriel experience his first real winter. He hadn't known cold like ours before, the kind that creeps into your bones and carves you from the inside out like a Ginsu knife.

It was in that cold that the protesters took to the streets.

Under a dim November sky, what should have been a routine sham election for a Moscow-appointed heir sparked the Orange Revolution. Every morning that month, Kyiv's students poured out of the Maidan Nezalezhnosti metro station to meet West Ukrainian bumpkins squatting in sleet-heavy tents on Khreshatyk; the ornate boulevard ended up hosting five madcap, subzero, outdoor weddings. Golden Gate and Cowboys morphed into soapboxes for American and Canadian children of the diaspora, returned home to hoist orange flags and practice stiff-from-the-box Ukrainian on babushkas with scant grins and faces carved from granite. A bizarre, beautiful carnival of revolt.

Before the Orange Revolution, Kyivites bitched about the wife-beating Afghan war veteran in the flat next door and the *bumzhiki* drinking themselves blind in Mariyinsky Park. Now we were having our first inferiority-free discussions of the European Union, and the Ukrainian Ministry of Finance was running vacancy ads in Kyiv's English-language weeklies. Even expats like Gabriel—that is, expats without Ukrainian hyphenated identities—could not ignore the fire in the air. For a stark beautiful moment, my tribe—by far one of the world's gloomiest—transformed into true believers. And I missed it all.

While orange banners snapped on my city's streets, I arranged shipments of .50-caliber machine guns with grim-faced men in Nazran and argued about the best markets for ivory and horn in Nairobi. When I did find myself in Kyiv—instead of braving the riot police in Independence Square and roaring "Yushenko *tak!*" with my countrymen—I snuggled with my foreign poet boy.

On a February night when the revolution already felt long gone, months-old Sky TV footage of protesters marched across the plasma TV in my high-rise.

"Yeah, yeah, yeah," Gabriel muttered, kicking his gnarled feet up onto the rosewood coffee table I'd snuck onto a shipment from Islamabad. "Ukraine has finally woken up."

He pointed the remote control at the satellite box.

I could have told Gabriel about my guilt at missing my country's moment. Explained how no matter how irrational it was, I partly blamed him for it. Or I could say something else. Something with teeth.

"American blacks lived under the boot longer. And more quietly."

"Wow, Tam, that's deep. Did you figure that out while standing in line for toilet paper with your granny?"

The insult didn't bother me as much as the fact that Gabriel didn't look me in the eyes when he said it.

"You're descended from unpaid labor too, you know," Gabriel continued, still avoiding my eyes. "Is there any real fucking difference between a serf and a slave?"

"Yep. A slave's a nigger." The word left a sickly sweet taste in my mouth, then hung in the air between us—rancid and ineradicable.

Gabriel—the conflicted boy—furious with his country for its racial history and with me for being unburdened by it. Yes, I spoke without the filter of American PC orthodoxy, but also without its weight. What kind of writer was he if he couldn't appreciate that? I never had reason to give Martin Luther King Jr. and the rest much thought. But did the success of their movement make its nonviolent approach less embarrassing? The murder of your children and flogging of your people was something—no matter the outcome—one *should* be ashamed of. A people born of capitalism who had shaped an ethos around their defeat. And, make no mistake, on the global stage all Americans are white.

Why couldn't Gabriel regard his country's racial history the same way most of us viewed the Soviet era? Something to be occasionally proud of and occasionally ashamed of, but mostly something that it was our generation's duty to move on from as quickly as possible.

"You cheap Ukrainian whore." Gabriel gnawed each word through clenched teeth. "For a hundred bucks, I can buy two of you for an hour. Today. Not two centuries ago. Tonight."

Gabriel strode dramatically to the door and fiddled ridiculously with the chain locks before finally getting it open. He slammed the heavy steel safe-room-style door behind him.

It took every ounce of my resolve not to storm out of the apartment after him, hurl another—crueler—insult. I knew which blades would reach marrow. Oh, yes. I knew. Menace him into stalking me back into the apartment and pinning my wrists to the pillow while I tore at his lips. He might just have had it in him. Then lie with him in bed until the room became too warm, and laugh at how the ice wind snapped at his bare ass when he cranked open the windows.

Instead I spun the lock and refastened the chains behind him. I leaned against the door and felt myself regaining control behind the steel.

I imagined Gabriel writing about his mad days in Kyiv, about the crazy, older Ukrainian woman he took up with once. A little boy, running away just to see if I'd follow.

I closed my eyes and saw Giga wiping wine from his mustache with the back of his hand.

"Now think hard, Tamarachka. Do I really need to meet this person?"

7 | Revolutions of All Colors

Part Two

Kyiv, Ukraine
March 2005

Gabriel

My eyes snap open.

Sunlight needles my face through the blinds.

Max's bathroom is five yards away but might as well be five hundred or five thousand. I grunt in a hail-Mary pelvic cinch. One way or another, within the next fifteen seconds, I'm going to be peeing. This is a fact, and that's just the way it is. I frantically dig into my jeans, scraping through stubbly pubic hair, and finally manage to flip out my junk. I drop my free hand off the couch, pat the floor until I find an empty beer bottle, and roll onto my side. Capturing the initial burst of urine and inching the bottle level under the flow is tricky, but I do all right. For the next few moments I'm overwhelmed by a pure, Zen-like feeling of release. Finally, I balance the warm receptacle onto the floor, grope for another bottle, sniff, and pour what I am fairly certain is tepid beer into my mouth.

The six days since Tamara dumped me have melded into an indistinct alcohol-fused mass. Max and I would lay down the first coat at Cowboys, head to III Nightclub in high spirits, and wash up at Kyiv's seediest strip joints at our most lecherous, leering at dead-eyed strippers until the birds chirped in the sunrise and I came to, dragon-retching into Max's toilet. We were drinking like the vodka sea was in danger of evaporating: clutching shot glasses like grudges, exchanging nods, and pouring liquor down our throats as if extinguishing something deep in our souls.

I was taking revenge. On Tamara for equating masculinity with all the traits she pretended to despise. On this racist country and its candy-ass revolution. On Frank for being so dead set against me dropping out of graduate school that returning to the States early would be an admission of failure. On the novel that refused to get written. On the dancing that never loved me as much as I loved it. On everything and everyone, including—especially—me. My Great Broken-Hearted Bender. Cliché? Yes indeedy. At least Max and I were doing it with flair. Our drinking was purposeful, the hangovers were postponed, and the eventual aftermath would be torrential.

When I open my eyes again, the shadows reveal that the sun's setting. Max is at his kitchen table. We're living like vampires.

"You pissed on the floor, young man." Max says, pointing at a dark patch on the mahogany without looking up from his reading.

"At least you don't have a carpet." The words scrape through my throat like bone on concrete. I cough into my fist and return my gaze to the ceiling.

"This intro reads like a Tolkien knockoff for black geeks," Max says.

I'd given him the first chapter of my novel before Tamara dumped me. This is his first time mentioning it.

"This opening sentence is timid, Gabs." Max buries the end of his pen in his beard. "Think of your opening sentence like banging a chick for the first time. Until you've established yourself, you gotta hit it with everything you've got. Initial sex and first sentences should leave an impression."

I don't have the energy to pretend I've slept with enough women to relate to this metaphor.

Max leans to one side and rips a long, mournful fart. "Actually, women are much more forgiving than readers." After a moment's contemplation, he adds, "Which is weird, because most readers of fiction are women."

Max writes literary fiction or, as he puts it, "perfect obituaries for people who never lived." With my speculative fiction, I was trying to do the same for people who couldn't have lived. In the end, we're both searching for the same thing: sentences clean as bone, smoothed into paragraphs that whistle.

"Please tell me you didn't seriously write a fantasy book about rings," Max says, rubbing his temples, then shouting, "Gabe! A fantasy book about rings! Please tell me you didn't do that!"

Besides half-drunk sojourns into Bladoonsky, where I attempted to teach while speaking as little as possible, I've spent the majority of the last 140 hours with Max. The sharpness of his sudden, exuberant excesses no longer shocks me.

"It's not about rings. It has a ring in it. And it's a crown on humans and elves." I've written an epic quest without a single dragon, but lots of elves. I've got a thing for elves. Everyone who writes fantasy has a thing for elves.

"It's a crown on humans and elves," Max mocks in a voice several octaves too high. "Jesus." He switches to Russian. "Tell me again how you never got laid in the States."

The connotations of the expression "*trahalsya*" are far nastier than "got laid." But I laugh anyway, mostly just to show Max I understand.

Max teaches Hebrew, English, and Russian at Bladoonsky. He also speaks Ukrainian. Tamara spoke all of those minus the Hebrew and plus French and German. Forced to chat with Max when they ran into each other at my apartment once— my life's version of ships passing in the night—Tamara asked him why he didn't teach Ukrainian. "Who would want to learn that shit?" Max asked, and I knew from his tone that it was, for him, a legitimate question.

Tamara and Max never liked each other, but their combined scorn of American linguistic laziness had a lot to do with me picking up Russian as quickly as I did. And there was a perverse gratification to learning Mr. Sergei's language—the language I'd received so much criticism in during my adolescence.

At the kitchen table, Max lights a joint the size of a jumbo crayon and, holding in a long drag, asks, "You want?"

The flickering green numbers on the microwave tell me it's 16:42. March 5, 2004. A Friday.

"Nah." I wave off the joint. "Let's get a drink."

Weed can't fuel this self-pity train. I need bourbon or vodka—some Hemingwayish liquor that I don't really like yet but am in the process of training myself to appreciate, as my father did and his father before him.

Max takes another toke.

I swing my legs off the couch and wait for the world to steady.

Max licks his fingers and squeezes the end of the joint. "A drink it is."

Tamara

The morning of March 5, 2004. My late father's birthday and what feels like the first real day of spring. Standing next to a crew chief in front of a hangar at Kyiv's Boryspil Airport, I watch gnarled Uzbeks and puffy-faced Byelorussians load crates of weapons and ammunition onto a Ukrainian chartered IL-76 transport plane. I have a job to do.

Here at the far end of the runway, away from the middle-class Ukrainian tourists and their early-morning discount flights to Sharm-El-Sheikh and Istanbul, the crew sweat through their striped undershirts while skittering around the cargo plane's yawning maw like ants.

This particular bunch is new to me, but I know IL-76 crews. Tomorrow this hodgepodge of former Soviet airmen could be packing their plane with antibiotics, Kenwood washing machines, ivory, or Johnnie Walker whiskey. Today it is weapons. During my eight years with Andreyi, we have used IL-76 crews as humanitarians, arms dealers, poachers, and drug dealers—sometimes all four in the same day. The trick is to never let them fly empty.

A gold-toothed airman, with a tan that ends abruptly at his wrists and neck, saunters toward the front of the hangar and, with one bear mitt, hoists two cans of Obolon in the direction of the crew chief and me. I wave off the perspiring can and glance at my Cartier La Dona. These boys might be airborne before seven a.m.

"That was fast," I tell the crew chief.

Instead of answering, the crew chief cracks open his beer, lifts it to his lips, and takes a long swallow. His eyes linger on me. Watching the crew chief from behind my sunglasses, a part of me hopes he won't say something that will force me to embarrass him. Another part of me—the part that wants to clarify to this pockmarked walrus his place in this deal, his place in my world—hopes that he will.

"Andreyi didn't tell you?" The crew chief glowers over his beer. "We're some of the best."

"Right." My gaze never leaves the plane. "What you're going to do now is have this one"—I jut my chin in the direction of the gold-toothed airman who delivered his beer—"get back to work so you and I can talk."

The crew chief takes a defensive swig, then sputters instructions to his crewmate about rechecking the cargo hold.

I wait until the airman is well on his way toward the plane before speaking. "Our previous partners were starting to disappoint."

"We'll get the stuff there on time." The crew chief glares at the plane.

I nod.

These former Soviet aircrews built legends out of exploits in dirt-floored bars in some of the dodgiest corners of the planet, and the last eight years have taught me what to expect of them—and not just servicewise. This crew chief's far from the first to mistake my lack of utter contempt for infatuation. So many of these guys seem to possess a subhuman allotment of decent impulses.

"Okay." I blink behind my sunglasses and snap my pen closed. "Call me from Wilson."

"Not Jomo Kenyatta?"

I lift my sunglasses onto my forehead and look directly at the crew chief. "No." Long pause. "You're flying into and out of Wilson." Everything on the Somalia contract flies through the smaller of Nairobi's two airports.

Something clicks in the crew chief's head. "Wilson. Yes, of course!"

"Wilson Airport." I replace my sunglasses on my nose. "Again, please give us a call after you arrive."

"Of course. Of course." Now the crew chief's wearing a sycophantic grin in a way that tells me he's used to the fit.

"Fine." I motion to our company's driver inside the hangar, just out of earshot.

I follow the driver to the car and slide onto the Mercedes's leather backseat, dropping my clipboard and purse next to me.

"We're going to the office," I say, massaging my forehead with my thumb and index finger. To hell with Gabriel.

Gabriel

The sun's almost set by the time we finally walk outside. I'm looking forward to a drink dulling my pangs of guilt at missing what must have been a beautiful day.

Max waves his hand at the cars zipping by on Patrice Lumumba Street outside his apartment. "Where are we going anyway?"

"Cowboys," I reply. "Where else?" Our Kyiv has shrunk to bars, Bladoonsky, and Max's apartment.

"Nope," Max says, catching my eyes. "Golden Gate."

"It's early for Golden Gate." No way am I hanging out in Tam's and my old go-to spot.

Max doesn't stop looking at me and then makes a show of a grand sigh. "Let's hear it for 'loyalty'!" He makes quotation marks with his fingers. "Okay. Cowboys it is. Again."

"It is loyalty, you know." I cringe at the whine in my own voice. "Cowboys is the second place . . ."

Max interrupts me in a voice more appropriate to a Chipmunks tune, " . . . a bartender got my drink for me before I asked."

I can't help but laugh.

"You act like that gap-toothed bartender of yours shakes martinis for us or something. The guy sets two middling Ukrainian beers on the counter when we walk in and suddenly I can't start my night anywhere else." Max slips into classroom mode and wags a finger at me to emphasize his seriousness. "We *are* going to Golden Gate afterward. I. Am. Fucking. Sick. Of. 111."

That gives me an hour to convince Max to stick to our tried-and-true crawl: Cowboys–111–horrible strip joint. I like my odds.

There's a midsized crowd in Cowboys. Mostly normal drinkers, folks out to shoot the shit on a Friday evening. But also a couple of the guys Max and I have started referring to as "the other motherfuckers." Motherfuckers who drink, as the saying goes, continually and to no obvious effect. Motherfuckers who don't consider beer alcohol. Motherfuckers with greater faith in vodka than conversation. Motherfuckers who haven't gone to bed sober in years. Twist-top bottles of wine the day before turning to vinegar. Walking cautionary tales of just how easy it is to stretch that one-time bender into another week, another month, another year. Motherfuckers whose every interaction with me seems underpinned by the question: "You one of us, kid, or just passing through?"

Oleg, the bartender—whose grin Max refers to as "a sparse, blackened testament to the United States' victory in the Cold War"—has two chilled glasses of Obolon on the counter by the time we pull up.

I don't say a word.

"All right. All right," Max says. "Are you paying this toothless bastard for the first round, or am I?"

Fuck you, Max. "I got it."

Max sips his immediately available beer, takes a deep breath, and turns to me. "You do realize that your relationship with Tamara was just about fucking, right?"

Okay. This is new.

"You know why you're an asshole, Max?" I've yet to meet someone who isn't interested in the answer to this question. "Because you assume people don't speak English until they prove otherwise."

"Judging by the number of functional teeth in this guy's mouth"—Max very intentionally does not look at Oleg as he speaks—"I would have to say no, Gabe, our friend here doesn't speak English."

"Real curious to hear how you're going to equate functional teeth with the ability to speak English."

"So now you're going to pretend you don't assume that someone missing more than half his teeth might be somewhat less than sophisticated?" he asks in his "your American pretentiousness is exhausting me" voice.

Max orders our first round of vodkas.

We watch in silence as Oleg pours.

"Okay. Fine," I say, annoyed by Max's entirely correct assumption that I'd crack first. "Why was my relationship with Tamara just about fucking?"

Max shrugs. "It's just how they do it. Ukrainian women, that is. They only hook up with blacks and Jews for the sex. The hypocrisy of these anti-Semitic Cossacks suddenly pretending to be liberal with all this Orange Revolution nonsense disgusts me. Truly. I swear, I prefer the Russians now. At least you know where you stand with them." Before I can get a word in, Max jams a finger into my sternum. "Save it. I'm an Eastern European Jew, man. I know the depths these motherfuckers can sink to."

"That's fucking ridiculous."

"Which part?" he asks, brightening, "The Ukrainian women thing?"

I nod.

"Well, it's less about them and more about us. It's just our place on the racial spectrum, young man. You guys more than us." Max raises two fingers to his unibrow. He might have even believed his own bullshit by this point. "But we're not far off. Shit. What about that one-nighter you bagged off with at the beginning of all this?" Max waves his hand around the bar, as I watch him flap his lips. "You try to act like this big feminist, but the truth is you love the game just as much as I do."

"You have no idea what you're talking about." The edge in my voice surprises me. "I couldn't even get it up with that girl the other night. You might be built for the 'game,' but I ain't."

Ukrainians say certain people's faces are just begging for a brick. At this moment Max has such a face.

I know the trope. Of course I know it. But I've never played the Mandingo spearman. Tamara and I were not that, and fuck Max for implying it.

"Tamara can have any man she wants," I say. "She chose me."

Max snorts.

Yeah, me, Max. Not you. What the hell could you know about a woman like Tamara? A woman whose very presence dizzied you?

Instead of asking either of these perfectly legitimate questions, I exhale slowly and push away from the bar. "I'm gonna take a piss. Wait for me on that shot."

Tamara

It's almost three in the afternoon when Andreyi calls me at the office to ask if I can pick up Sasha from school at four.

I cut off my boss midapology. "Of course. No problem. You know I love to chat with Sasha." There aren't many people Andreyi trusts with his son. "I'm going in that direction to my mother's this afternoon anyway."

I arrive at Bladoonsky with the driver and company car just as children start pouring out of the building.

On the sidewalk next to the car, I hardly get the chance to tap out a cigarette before I spot Sasha.

"There's my man!" I say, realizing just how much I've been hoping to run into Gabriel.

Sasha gives me a closed-mouthed grin, before ducking into the car.

During the drive out to Kharkovsky—the suburb where my mother lives, one of Kyiv's least prestigious addresses—I ask Sasha about his favorite teacher.

"He wasn't at school today," Sasha says, hand hovering around his lips. "Tell him I said 'hi' when you see him."

"I'll be sure to pass on the little prince's greetings," I say.

He wasn't at school? Gabriel wouldn't have done anything stupid, would he? No. No, of course not.

Sasha nods. His most recent thing—nodding and shaking his head, talking into his palms, and smiling with just his lips—anything to hide the braces.

I place my finger on Sasha's chin. "What'd I tell you about that? Don't hide your smile, *lapochka*. They win when you hide your smile."

Sasha looks up at me, eyes pure green pools. "Gabe says my teeth make me fierce."

"Well." I swallow the longing welling up in my chest. "Gabriel's right."

My phone buzzes in my bag. I flip open the device, then feel my shoulders drop. +254. A Kenyan number.

I glance at my watch. Almost four thirty. "You guys made good time. I trust you're at the right airport . . . ?"

"Okay, Tamara. You've made your point." The crew chief bristles through the phone line. "We just checked into Samra"—a hotel not far from Wilson Airport where I stayed during my last trip to Nairobi—"and the boys are already out and about. We're all set to fly first thing in the morning."

"What about the other stuff?"

"The other stuff is still waiting for us at the airport in Mogadishu," the crew chief responds.

The "other stuff" is fresh horn and ivory, hacked off black rhinos and elephants in Kenya's Tsavo National Park, driven overland to the port city of Lamu, and shipped up the coast to Mogadishu. The crew will drop the weapons in Mog and fly the "other stuff" to Hanoi. Given the prices tusk and horn demand in Asia—and the fact that we are trading small arms for the ivory straight up—this is set to be our most profitable deal to date.

"Okay. Keep an eye on your crew and give me a call in the morning."

"Fine," the crew chief says.

The Mercedes pulls up to the patchwork courtyard in front of my mother's building.

"Come on, Sasha." I close my phone. "The sooner we say hello to my momma, the sooner we're off to the stables."

I pause and very nearly tell Sasha that today would have been my father's sixty-sixth birthday, then decide not to.

The Soviet-era apartment blocks on Kyiv's outskirts are massive, cheerless structures. So huge that, for ease of reference, each individual communal foyer—*pod'yezd*—is included in the address. My mother, Luba, lives in Kyiv's Kharkovsky suburb: #31 Revutskogo Street, 2nd pod'yezd, apartment 12L. She shares the twelfth floor with two widows, a doctor, and a whore.

Sasha and I walk through the quartet of terrifying corrugated metal giraffes and horses on the playground in front of the second pod'yezd. We spot one of Luba's neighbors, the doctor, Zenja, slumped on a park bench next to the orange and pink jungle gym, eyes closed, head bobbing to a tune only he can hear. Even during the worst of winter, a few of Revutskogo's dispirited men can always be found here, under the playground animals' steel gaze, raising plastic bottles of vodka.

I pull Sasha along by the hand.

Zenja lives with his mother, one of the twelfth-floor widows. He finished medical school during the same spring I completed my first degree, just in time to enter a society in which bilingual secretaries had a better chance of earning a living wage than cardiologists. I struggle to reconcile the exceptionally bright teenager—whom I had a crush on growing up—with the man I now see on park benches, clutching bottles and glaring at me with the eyes of a boy whose intelligence had so exceeded his circumstances.

I tap in the door code to the building. The scent of unfiltered cigarettes, garlic, and vinegar greets us in the foyer—a smell I grew up with and always associate with melancholy. The groundskeeper grunts a greeting over his shoulder, then continues rummaging through the foyer closet. I usher Sasha into the lift and push the button for the twelfth floor. Someone has scribbled "I love" in Russian, followed by "Cort" in English on the control panel. The lift jerks to the twelfth floor.

What's "Cort"? A nickname? Slang for a drug? A body part?

On the twelfth floor, I walk to my mother's door and hesitate, my finger hovering over the buzzer. Sasha looks up at me, grinning with all his rows of metallic teeth. *Bozhe.* The kid does look fierce when he smiles.

It's a gift really, the way Gabriel sees the world. All wasted on silly fantasy stories, instead of telling *his* stories. Those I would read. Would've read.

I press the doorbell, and we listen to the faint buzz within the apartment. We stare at the door for a few moments and then glance at each other. I hold the doorbell for a good fifteen seconds, knock, and finally fumble through my purse for the keys.

I slip off my heels before stepping onto the dark, polished oak floor, worrying, as usual, about sliding in my stockinged feet. But these were the floors Luba wanted, so these are the floors I got her. We step through the hallway into the kitchen, dotted with pictures of me: graduating from law school; half running, half hopping on a pebbled beach in Odessa; posing next to a plane in a hangar in Beirut.

We squint at the sunlight flooding through the floor-to-ceiling windows and find the triumvirate of widows that make up Luba's inner circle huddled around the glass-topped kitchen table, scooping jam into their tea. The renovations I paid for haven't left much of the apartment's original architectural detail. The place is now airy and open. Still, the triumvirate clusters in corners, as if at any moment the space might revert to its original, cramped Soviet style.

"Tamarachka! Sashenka!" they cry in unison.

"*Privet! Privet!*" I reply, my enthusiasm not entirely false.

Sasha fights his way through the cheek-pinching and hugs into the living room.

"It's okay if I play Game Boy?" he asks, then plops cross-legged on the floor facing the window without waiting for an answer.

"We can't stay long, Momma. Sasha's meeting his aunt and cousins at the stables."

The ladies shuffle around in their chairs to make room for me.

"Of course, my dear, of course," Luba says, pushing the tin of sweets in my direction. "You can never stay long."

I flinch, watch my mother's ample but resiliently beautiful pale face. The cigarettes in my purse are calling me by my first name. Instead, I reach for a chocolate.

Parrying the triumvirate's onslaught of concentrated depression and unsolicited advice is like treading water in a pool of, not sharks exactly, more like formidably stout, aggressively helpful porpoises. I fire off responses like bursts from an automatic rifle:

"*Nyet*, Maria Andreyivna, I never heard that a little sugar will keep a rose alive longer."

"*Da*, Momma, I have been dressing warmly—this spring weather could turn at any moment!"

"*Da-nyet*, Nataliya Vasilivna! The only 'special man' in my life right now is playing video games in the living room."

Sasha looks up from his Game Boy, face scrunched in disgust. I give him a "sorry, kid, but I'm drowning here" look, then raise a finger to the triumvirate to answer my buzzing mobile.

"Hello?" I say into the phone, as the freight train of the triumvirate's conversation chugs on without me.

"There was some trouble at the place next to the hotel," the crew chief says.

I am well aware of the sort of establishment neighboring the Samra hotel.

"So someone didn't pay"—I almost say "for a prostitute," before remembering where I am—"for the damage?"

"Worse. The Kenyan police are here. One of my boys is upstairs, butt naked, dead as a doornail, with an empty package of generic Nigerian Viagra at his bedside."

"*Vot blyad*," I say, forgetting about my mother and using the Russian equivalent of "what the fuck"—which is literally "whore."

"*Vot blyadee* is probably more accurate," the crew chief corrects me, changing the noun to the plural.

I imagine the airman's heart giving out at his moment of ecstasy. Swarmed by Kenyan whores, huge grin frozen under one of those circus-strong-man mustaches, permanently stiff prick pressed against his paunch in a final solemn salute to the sky he loved so well.

I snicker. Gabriel would've seen the humor in all this.

"They're still 'investigating.'" The crew chief's voice drops quotation marks around the word. "Hopefully our boy didn't have anything on him that will raise eyebrows."

I am no longer snickering.

Arrest isn't a concern; losing a shipment—and a lot of cash—is. We've had caches "go missing" before. And this shipment is particularly extravagant. In addition to the usual guns and ammunition it includes rocket-propelled grenade launchers, C-4, and even some "dual purpose" equipment: night vision goggles and flak jackets.

"Okay. Well." I expected a quick "the stuff ships tomorrow"–type conversation, not this. "So, you'll move everything tonight?"

"Just like that, huh?" The crew chief sulks.

"What do you mean?" I ask.

"Oh, nothing," the crew chief says. "I'll take care of it."

I hold the phone in silence. One, two, three, four, five, six, seven, eight, nine, ten, eleven.

The crew chief snorts something about getting in touch soon and hangs up. Wait thirty seconds and the other party will almost always say something. The only practical advice I picked up in law school.

"Work?" Luba asks.

"Yes, Momma." I place my phone next to a teacup. "It's always work."

One of the widows—Nataliya Vasilivna, a woman who has never stopped referring to Gorbachev as "the one who destroyed us"—is in the middle of affecting a thick-tongued Ukrainian accent to mock the Orange Revolution protesters.

The triumvirate talked a lot of politics during my visits that winter, and I hadn't always managed to stay out of it. Luba's voice always carried a twinge of hurt during these conversations. In the Soviet Union's ethnic mash-up, Russians like my mother thought of Ukrainians as favored little brothers and being spurred by family stings. The "Orange Revolution" was a stark reminder that Russians and Ukrainians are not one tribe. And if the weapons trade has taught me nothing else, it is the lengths humans will go to for their tribes.

Luba drops her hand on mine before I can respond to Nataliya Vasilivna's taunt.

"No politics today," she says. "Okay, lapochka?"

I hold my mother's gaze.

In this kitchen, at twenty-three years old and in my first year of law school, I decided to get the abortion. On the forty-five-minute bus ride from school to my parents' place in Kharkovsky, I sat, hands neatly folded in my lap while chairing a frenzied internal debate. Would I drop out of school? Marry the one-night fling who'd knocked me up? Remain single and arrange some kind of coparenting thing? Weekend custody for the dad? How had a microscopic collection of cells in my uterus suddenly morphed into a tiny person with a vote on my weekend plans? And anyway, how good could my kid's weekend custody deal possibly be in comparison to the pain in the ass of having to see that dolt once a week? *Chert poberi.* I'd discovered too late that my one-nighter had a heart like a split pea and the personality of a walking, talking pustule. I was terrified.

I burst into my parents' kitchen, humid with the smell of simmering onions.

"Stew for Papa's hunting trip this weekend." Luba smiled, strands of graying hair sweat-plastered to her forehead.

"Papa's going hunting at Andreyi's dacha this weekend?" I asked. "Again?"

"Your father and Andreyi have been best friends since their time in the army." Luba didn't look up from the carrots on the chopping board. The knife, an extension of her beefy arm, slowed only to push the green tufts off the mahogany board. Would I ever command anything so well as Luba did a kitchen?

"Besides," Luba continued, "his birthday's this weekend."

I feared how naturally it came to her, devoting all her time and energy to a man who barely noticed. Even then I knew what my future boss and father got into on those weekends at the dacha. The drinking. The women. It's a wonder Giga's heart gave out before his conscience. I searched Luba's face for a flicker of resentment, a speck of pride. I wanted to join Momma in grudging acceptance, maybe even offer a commiserate shoulder. But studying Luba's unflinching, fleshy face, I realized she needed neither.

"Get the pot from up under the sink, lapochka."

I corrected her Russian. "From under the sink."

"Hmmmmm?"

"Not from 'up under' the sink. From under the sink."

"Of course, lapochka. Of course."

Luba couldn't even get our native tongue right.

I never told her about the warm feeling of pure goodness emanating from my womb. Or about the power of knowing whatever came next was my choice and mine alone. Watching my mother's face—that peasant's face—I knew that we would never have that conversation. I got the abortion that weekend and never told a soul.

I turn to Sasha, on his stomach, in the living room, face bathed in the Game Boy's artificial light. My boy would be about the same age now. It would have been a boy. I know it. Gabriel—conflicted, heart-too-big-for-his-own-good Gabriel—is the only person I ever want to tell how incredibly strong and unspeakably sad I felt at that moment, eleven years ago today.

My phone buzzes again. The office.

"We have to go, Momma."

"Okay, lapochka."

"See you soon."

She squeezes my hand and after a moment I squeeze back.

Downstairs in front of the pod'yezd, a small crowd of the neighborhood retirees and un- and underemployed are gathered around the doctor's park bench. Sasha and I push our way through the crowd. The doctor is supine, a line of pink saliva stretching from his cracked lips to a puddle of crimson-tinged vomit under the park bench.

I raise my hand to my mouth and take a step forward.

"Don't," the groundskeeper says, placing a hand on my shoulder. "He's *sdoh*." Croaked. An ugly word used to describe carrion. "I've already called for an ambulance."

I shrug off the groundskeeper's paw. But the gray leather of Zenja's face, crisscrossed with spidery blue veins, does look putrid, like something already hard to imagine having ever been alive. I cover Sasha's eyes and guide him to the edge of the crowd.

I tap out a text to my mother. *Zenja is dead. Please stay upstairs, there's nothing for you to do down here.*

Another member of the triumvirate, Maria Andreyivna, accompanies Nataliya Vasilivna downstairs.

Nataliya drops to her knees next to the park bench with a wounded animal wail of despair. For a long moment she remains there, shuddering with tears, and many of us look away.

While my former crush approached drinking himself to death as if it had been his job, Nataliya had been in a mourning holding pattern, watching her son circle the drain. I hope that now, after all, Nataliya finds some peace.

"Let's go," I tell Sasha.

He nods.

The ambulance arrives as I nudge the top of Sasha's head under the roof of the Mercedes. Ambulances always seem to arrive quickly when there's no expectation that the medics can do any good. Dressed in blue coveralls, the two medics shove Nataliya aside and pack the corpse into the off-white UAZ van. Nataliya climbs into the ambulance behind them without looking back.

I drop Sasha at the stables with his aunt.

Before I can walk back to the car, he seizes my hand. "Don't forget to tell Gabriel I said 'hi,' okay?"

I call the crew chief from the car. He confirms that several manifests are missing from the plane's ledger. Why someone would take copies of a plane's manifest to a Kenyan whorehouse was anybody's guess, but it seems that is exactly what the airman had done. Idiot. Has anyone even contacted his family yet?

I focus, refusing to let this airman evolve into a person like Zenja. A person with a profession he loved and a mother who will wail at his death. I have a job to do.

"What did Andreyi say?" the crew chief asks.

I blink at the sparkling Dnieper River as the Mercedes speeds across the Moskovskyi Bridge on the way back to the city. "Move everything tonight."

The line goes silent.

"You haven't spoken to Andreyi about this, have you?" the crew chief says at last.

No, you moron, I haven't. My job is to put out the fires before Andreyi smells the smoke.

"Does it matter?" I say. "Listen. The chances of us losing that shipment increase with every moment of you sitting on your hands in Nairobi."

"It's risky to move the stuff now," the crew chief says in a voice of indulgent exasperation. "I want to know what Andreyi has to say about this."

"There's a reason you don't have Andreyi's phone number. *I* am telling you: move the stuff. Do it now."

"Yeah, it's just my ass on the line."

"Your ass will be fine. It's our balance sheets I'm concerned about."

"Okay. I'll call you tonight," the crew chief says. "If we lose this one, it's on you."

I exhale directly into my mobile's receiver, then speak very slowly, enunciating each syllable as if speaking to someone with an intellectual deficit. "Move. Everything. Tonight."

Gabriel

We end up at 111.

As I wade through the sweaty density and thumping Euro-techno to the toilets, a girl's eyes meet and lock on mine from the dance floor. Her makeup shimmers in the club's flashing, oscillating lights, and we communicate something warm and sincere, something intensely human. Then we both look away.

That's when I take the first punch. I raise my hands to my face and stagger into someone who immediately shoves me in the back. I flay into the crowd on the dance floor and feel, for a horrific moment, surrounded by ghouls, assaulted by the nightclub itself.

I spin just as Max lands a perfect left in what must have been a tidy one-two combination. I ground my weight on the moons of my feet and swing on a bloated fellow who appears to be with the guy Max is pummeling. My fist connects solidly with lip and chin. Exhilaration floods the alcohol from my veins. I swing twice more, wildly, connecting only once: an unsatisfyingly mushy blow to my guy's soft gut.

Then Max is bundling me up the stairs. Our attackers hang back, cursing. One, I'm assuming the poet of the bunch, invites us to ride a dick while whistling.

"Time to go, Gabs!"

Halfway up the staircase, I see why Max is suddenly in such a rush. Leather-jacketed, asp-wielding orcs are making their way from the bar toward us. We dart up the stairs and tumble onto the street. We barrel toward the end of Pobedy Square, as if the gates of Hades have been loosed at our backs.

Max's hand locks on my elbow.

I stop, jerking free of his grasp.

Max stares at me. "You okay?"

"Fuck those racist thugs! Fuck this country!" My voice cracks. "Fuck Tamara!" I turn away from Max, terrified of the tears welling up in my eyes. No. God, no. Please. Not in front of Max. I slump onto the curb.

Max drops down next to me. He pats his body until locating a joint and lighter. Cars, streetlights, and billboards flash blurrily. Max takes a couple puffs, then taps his elbow against mine, offering me the unlit end.

"To Ukrainian thugs and black romantics." Max laughs, and—I have to hand it to the guy—his voice is not one bit unkind.

I take a long pull.

"The world's got enough thugs, Gabs. Romantics are rare."

I pass the joint back to Max and press my palms against my eyes. I want to thank him but don't trust my voice. I exhale, blowing the type of forceful raspberry that's meant to change the subject.

"That eye's gonna be three different colors tomorrow," Max says.

I touch my face, only then noticing the dull painful throb. At least the skin's intact.

"Ain't nothing." I thumb my nose like a prizefighter. "I learned to take a punch before I learned to take a compliment."

Max smirks. "Your dad?"

"All the good ones are from my dad." I pat my face with my fingertips. "Racist fucking Cossacks."

"Come on, man. Don't do that. Maybe you smiled at one of their girls. Maybe I banged one of their girls last week. Bar fights aren't supposed to make sense. That's why they're so fucking great." Max takes another drag, excitement flushes on his face, and he leaps to his feet. "Wake up, Gabs! Look at us, man! It doesn't get better than this! These are the greatest days of our fucking lives!"

I'm laughing too hard to hear the rest of his speech. But that's okay because I know that no matter what nonsense spewed out of his mouth what he was really saying was that he loved me. I loved him too.

Max's pupils latch onto mine like a tractor beam.

"Golden Gate?" he asks.

I hoist myself to my feet and dust off my jeans.

"I can't think of one reason why not."

Tamara

From the office, I adjust clearances, calm clients in Hanoi, and affect half a dozen bank transfers.

I glance at my silent mobile, nestled between binders on my desk. Gabriel's nuts if he thinks I'll be the first to reach out.

When my girlfriends call wanting to meet at a new Greek restaurant downtown, I insist on Golden Gate.

I order the most expensive vodka on the menu, and we are on our fourth shots when my phone buzzes. +252. Somalia.

"Stuff's delivered," the crew chief says. "We're happy."

I realize just how much tension has been pent in my shoulders.

"You're taking off for Hanoi?"

"Yep. Just finished loading the other stuff."

"Let's hope those pharmaceuticals will be ready for pickup in Vietnam," I say. "Otherwise you'll be flying back to Kyiv empty."

"Rules were made to be broken, my dear. Worse comes to worse, you two can pay us for the difference. With the profit on this deal you certainly can afford it."

The line goes quiet. One, two, three, four, five, six, seven, eight.

Finally, the crew chief continues, "You were right not to push our luck with the Kenyans."

"Always trust your luck, but never push it." Another of Giga's lines.

The crew chief snorts. *"Molodets."* Atta girl.

I toss the mobile onto the table and scoop up the vodka bottle.

"Work?" one of my girlfriends asks.

"Always work." I refill our shot glasses. "I'm going to dance tonight."

Gabriel

Tamara's on the dance floor, holding the hems of her skirt and shaking her hips, eyes closed, honey-blonde locks swaying to a reggae chant.

Ohh yeah . . . Ohhh yeah . . . Ohhh yeah . . .

She pulls her hair away from her face, lifts her chin, and looks directly at me. My goddess of war.

Tamara

I open my eyes to Gabriel walking in the door. His face swollen like a dinner roll, with a blossoming black eye, and a look not at all gentle.

The music continues, but I stop dancing.

Gabriel

I place a hand on Max's shoulder but don't break from Tamara's eyes.

"I'll see you later, bruh."

"Go with God, young man."

Tamara

Gabriel walks toward me on the dance floor.

Da, Papa, you would have needed to meet this one.

Gabriel

She clutches my face with both hands and kisses me on the mouth. A cold vodka kiss.

The air squeezes out of my lungs.

I want to time capsule this moment to my grandkids with a note attached: "This is what love is supposed to feel like. Don't accept less."

8 | The Tap Cascade

Jersey City, New Jersey
May 2006

> A preference for questionable and terrifying things
> is a symptom of strength.
> —Friedrich Nietzsche, *The Will to Power:*
> *An Attempted Transvaluation of All Values*

ALL OF IT'S A BLUR until the first punch. The music, the lights, the crowd, the walk to the ring, the introductions, approaching the ref, touching gloves—you don't remember any of it except that first punch. In your first bout, you beat a fighter within an inch of his life. Not just a man, a fighter: someone who eats clean, doesn't drink, worships at the altar of the Fight God. The first punch you land decimates a barrier. The second blasts lightning through your veins. The third's the last you remember. Then the ref is wrenching you off the battered body. Roaring. Victorious.

You win your first three fights with knockouts. Coaches can't teach raw power. Either a guy has it or he doesn't. You

This chapter originally appeared as "The Tap Cascade" in *Southern Humanities Review*, vol. 53.1, 2020.

have it. Promoters notice. Power punchers fill seats. The venues get bigger. The money gets better.

Your fourth fight is with Sam Heenan, an up-and-comer from Iowa. There's no tape on him (really YouTube footage nowadays, but everyone still calls it tape). Your coach, Pat Kedzie, predicts that Heenan will go straight to the mat—fighters from Iowa always do. You wrestled in high school. You know that some of the best grapplers on the planet come out of Iowa. There and Brazil. Proof that the Fight God has a sense of humor.

You stand in the ring across from Heenan, not listening to the ref's instructions. You stare at each other without malice or derision—a silent physical appraisal. Heenan's a lanky white dude with cauliflower ears and a nose like a man who worked the docks two centuries ago. You're fighting at 195, 5 pounds heavier than him. He's six three, two inches taller than you, but your reach is about the same.

You touch gloves and manage one glancing punch before Heenan rushes and you both tumble to the mat. Then it's all violent and subtle shifts of weight—squirming, reaching, keeping your head above water while trying to pull Heenan under. A complex game of kinetic chess.

"Breathe, Simon!" Pat shouts from your corner. "Goddamn it, breathe!"

Calm down. Shift. Work. Move. Calm down.

You're in a good spot, latched on his back. You dig your heels into Heenan's crotch as he claws for space between your forearm and his carotid artery.

His fingers slip.

You snarl, lock, and pull in that near-orgasmic moment when the crook of your elbow finds his Adam's apple.

You know what Heenan's feeling; you've been there in training more times than you care to admit. The tap cascade: that all-consuming panic, those fireflies on the periphery of your vision, and then, finally, the tap. Surrender and momentary relief stalked by anger, disgust, and disappointment.

You roll off Heenan and bring your gloves to your face, the roar of the fans swallowing you whole. You've rappelled from helicopters, jumped out of perfectly good airplanes, and everyone who's ever shot at you missed. But nothing beats this: pure adrenaline on tap.

The Heenan fight shuts up your detractors.

"Yeah, he's got that power punch—he can hit, but can he fight?"

No more. Fighters who never looked your way at Razor— Jersey City Razor, your gym—now nod when you enter.

"That's Simon Moten, an up-and-comer."

You nod back but keep your mouth shut. You're older than many of these fighters, but not in gym years. And that's the only time that counts.

❁

You were contracting with one of the fly-by-night, Blackwateresque firms in Mogadishu when you received Pat's email.

Were you serious about fighting MMA one day? Where'd you say you placed in Oklahoma's 6A division back in high school? What year was that? You still in shape?

Long before Mog, back at Camp Vance in Afghanistan, you'd served on a mixed team of SEALs, FBI Hostage Rescue, Army Civil Affairs, and members from "other government agencies." You'd been a rookie air force PJ, and Pat, a redheaded grizzly bear of a master gunnery sergeant who talked nonstop about MMA, had been the team's most seasoned EOD tech. Waaaay back in the day—between pre-9/11 deployments—Pat had fought, managed, and coached. Most guys did it on the side back then. As a real sport MMA has only been around since '93 or so—a little over a decade. Pat was one of those early MMA enthusiasts who'd done everything in the sport except make money at it. Retired from the corps, Pat had returned to his native Jersey City to open a gym and manage a stable of fighters full time.

You took Michael up on his standing offer to move into his place in New York. Unlike the other guys on Pat's roster, you didn't have to fight every three or four weeks, hunting for purses. Between the military and contracting in Somalia, you had plenty to live on and even a chunk of change put away for your kid, Marlon. You still haven't met Marlon. Thanks to the Fight God, you hardly even think of him.

You told everyone that you took the contracting job in Mogadishu for the money. But that's a lie. You took the job in Mog because—after Afghanistan—you knew you could lose yourself in Somalia. War zones are great like that. Turned out, fighting was even better. The Fight God doled out that same sublime, single-minded clarity of purpose, and victory in the ring was clean and pure. All the Fight God demanded was a life shorn of complex human relationships, alcohol, drugs, and pleasure in food. In return, he shrouded you in his little sect, made you difficult for the rest of the world to find. And that's exactly what you wanted.

※

You train, eat, sleep, and repeat—interspersed with Internet porn sessions. And repeat.

"There aren't any bonus points for making yourself miserable, Simon." Michael tells you. "Let's go out."

"Not tonight." Your standard refrain.

Michael decides to stay in with you.

"So, we weren't even halfway through the starter when it occurred to me that Jose was trying to get me drunk." Jose is Michael's new boss. "Sy! Simon! Are you listening?"

Michael's in the kitchen. You're lying on the couch. It's not a big apartment.

"Hmmm? Sorry. Sounds like Jose has a thing for overeducated, skinny-ass, high-yella black dudes."

You confirmed Michael's bisexuality years ago when you were at his place on leave from Hurlburt Field, just after your first deployment. Michael had just moved into the two-bedroom walkup in Manhattan's West Village that you now shared. The conversation had been about blow jobs.

"Until you've had one from a dude"—Michael closed his eyes and shook his head as if he smelled something sumptuous—"you haven't had one."

Now, in the living room, you're locked in a staring contest with Josephine, Michael's tuxedo-patterned cat. Jo wiggles into Michael's lap at every opportunity, but if you lay a finger on her she convulses like she's possessed.

"I'm going to eat this cat one day."

Michael sighs theatrically. "In the end we all turn into our mothers."

Your mom barely looked up from the paper when you asked for a dog back in high school. You even had Frank speak to Ettie about it. "Son, there are very few things in this life that I can say with absolute certainty," Frank told you afterward, laughing. "This is one of them: you ain't getting a dog."

In the apartment, Josephine tightropes the couch's armrest while holding your gaze like a dare. Living with Josephine has convinced you that if domestic cats grew to the size of domestic dogs, they would definitely kill people. Regularly.

"On my second tour, our interpreter went nuts for the dogs." You break away from Jo's glare to face Michael. He nods—you've told him about your friend Wes before. "Dude became more of a dog handler than the dog handlers. Wes used to say that working dogs outrank their handlers. The highest-ranking handler was an army sergeant. So that made Hal, Wes's favorite Belgian shepherd, a staff sergeant. Everyone would tell Wes that when him and Hal fucked it was a hat trick: homosexuality, bestiality, and fraternization."

Michael shakes his head. "Sometimes you sound nostalgic for that good old casual military homophobia."

"That and the casual sexism," you say, smiling. "Wes always said that female dogs are more loyal than males." You gesture at the unamused Jo. "Must go for cats too."

"Probably."

"Pat's bringing in a female trainer to work with us next month."

"Huh. If nothing else it'll be good for you to spend some time around a nondigital woman." Michael laughs at his own joke.

You shrug. Pain shoots through your shoulder, and you adjust the ice pack you're balancing there. Michael watches you from the doorway to the kitchen.

"Lil' love tap from Yunior," you explain. "You met him. One of the dudes in my stick."

Michael removes his glasses.

Oh, God. Not another heart-to-heart.

"Why do this to yourself?" Michael asks with a sincerity that at once breaks your heart and demands that you fuck with him.

"Because. It's the best. Fucking. Job. In the world." Then with far more earnestness in your voice than you intended. "I'm 4–0, Michael. I'm good at this." Your first time saying this out loud. Seems you're starting to believe all Pat's talk about a title.

"Hmmm." Michael rubs the bridge of his nose. "When're you going to see Marlon?" Dude's not even subtle about inserting the kid into conversations lately.

"After this fight." Your tone is so sincere that you almost convince yourself. "I'm going back to Oklahoma after my next fight."

Michael returns to the kitchen. You hear him rummaging in the fridge.

"I don't see you rushing back to Oklahoma, Michael."

"I don't have a son there."

"You have a mom and dad there."

"So do you," Michael responds immediately.

He's right. Frank's always treated you like one of his boys.

"Besides, your Antoine"—Michael's voice sours at the mention of your hometown—"wasn't my Antoine."

"Yeah, well, I made your Antoine mine, didn't I?"

Michael closes the refrigerator door with a flourish, places the back of his hand on his forehead, and strikes the pose of a heroine swooning. "My knight in shining armor!" He rolls his eyes. "Grow up, Sy. You need to meet your son."

You smile at how Michael has grown into himself.

Jo hisses as if she's just read your mind.

"Jesus. Evil motherfucker."

Michael laughs. "You talking to me or her?"

Your fifth fight is in Japan. Backstage, you feel yourself smirking as Pat finishes one of his painstakingly prepared prefight speeches.

"We should be thankful to be part of this fraternity of blood and pride and sacrifice," Pat tells you with a straight face. It's impossible not to love this man.

The fans yell in stilted English during your walk to the ring in Tokyo.

"Go forward!"

"Do not falter!"

They remind you how true fight fans, including the fighters themselves, respect anyone who dares all in the ring. How a fighter's reputation is not just how much he wins, but also how he loses.

By the end of the first round, Dmitry Kanaris, "the Greek," has you blowing burgundy snot bubbles and holding your chin at a ninety-degree angle to peek out of a painfully ballooned left eye.

Pat shoves a swab into your left nostril and pinches the other with his thumb. "Inhale."

The medicinal, slightly metallic tang of Vaseline, Adrenalin Chloride, and blood fills your mouth. You spit into the bucket. Your nasal cavity goes a brittle, crusty dry.

"Good." Pat tips some water into your mouth and then slaps you twice with a black-latex-gloved hand. "Now stop giving him clean shots."

Kanaris is stronger than you and just as technically proficient. But you spent more time blowing sweat off your nose than "the Greek" did. Conditioning allows you to be tougher, gives you the option not to quit.

Humans rarely rise to the level of their expectations; usually they fall to the level of their habits, their training. Some guys figure this out on their high school wrestling teams. Others figure it out in Muay Thai camps. Still others during Hell Week. You got lucky in life by figuring it out early. When and how to listen to your body. And—just as important, maybe even more so—when and how to utterly ignore it: how to shut the fuck up and buck the fuck up.

In the ring, you stand fast and trade blows in a crimson haze, until you own space in that motherfucker's soul.

Few men know exactly how much they are capable of. On that September evening in front of a crowd of true fight fans in Tokyo, Kanaris helps you find out. When the ref lifts your hand, no one in the venue—not even Kanaris—doubts the decision.

✿

You limp into Razor a week later with the type of postfight soreness that's become less physical pain and more simply a physical fact of your existence now—like how many times a week you should shave your head.

"Make friends with the pain," the Fight God whispers, "and you'll never be alone."

It's early. Two rows of heavy bags dangle like strange fruit at one end of the gym. Pat's in the office at the other end. You drop your gym bag and collapse onto the mat, bathed in autumn sunshine from Razor's high panoramic windows. The scent of cleaning detergent singes the hair in your nostrils.

Five Ws—including three knee-buckling kayos—and no Ls. Next up is Malcolm McKay, a black southpaw Brit with a reputation as a banger.

"This guy's big time," Pat told you in the hotel in Tokyo, with his hand over the telephone receiver. "This win would put us on the next level."

And McKay knew it. You were getting an opportunity. He was getting a 70 percent take.

Malcom McKay. Even the guy's name sounded like a super-hero's alter ego. Would he go toe to toe? Straight to the mat? You've tried to stop obsessing about your opponents. Focus on your game, you tell yourself, not his. But it's no use.

Later, when Michael found the picture of McKay taped on the bathroom mirror in the apartment, he just shook his head. "Like a twelve-year-old with a crush."

"Balanced people don't accomplish great things," you tell him.

"Don't you feel even slightly embarrassed when you say things like that?"

You don't. You *want* fighting to crowd everything else out of your life. To navigate the gap between good and great, you have to make choices. That's what Gabs always got that his older brother didn't: balance doesn't work. None of the greats—at anything—were balanced. Over the next couple months, you'll see McKay sparring while you're taking a water break, watching tape while you're sleeping. He's getting better. What the fuck are you doing?

You open an eye and watch Pat walk toward you—barefoot, smiling, and far beyond the point of diminishing returns when it comes to muscle. Just a crazy yoked, redheaded Viking motherfucker whose presence sends your mind reeling for synonyms for scary.

Pat squats next to you on the mat. "Boy, you look like your asshole is sucking buttermilk."

You laugh, almost ask, and then decide you prefer that that particular metaphor remain vague. "I'm hurting. But ready to get back to work."

"I got some tape on McKay for us to watch later."

You roll onto your side, prop your head up on your elbow. "How's he look?"

"Beatable." Pat lifts your chin with his finger. The Kanaris fight left a nasty mat burn on your cheek. "Watch that, we don't want it to get infected."

You nod and sit up to a cross-legged position.

Pat straightens, and his knees pop like a Rice Krispies commercial. "My advice to you is to put off reaching my age as long as possible."

You laugh. Pat gives you this advice at least once a week.

"That new trainer's coming in to take you boys through the paces this morning."

You catapult to your feet Bruce Lee–style and pat your belly, making a constipated face. "Lemme insert a marine recon team real quick and get stretched."

Pat shows you fangs, then laughs when you dart away.

Fighters begin trickling in. There are usually eight or nine of you for the early-morning session. It's a motley group: firefighters, street toughs, cops, two Rutgers graduate students. A year ago, you started calling the morning session "your stick"—like at Jump School. The other guys loved it. Most days, Pat trains with your stick. An amazing feat, given how hard the guy parties.

The first time you and Michael went out with Pat—more than a year ago now—you spent an hour beforehand talking down your trainer/manager.

"Pat's a nice guy. But a pretty simple motherfucker, if you know what I mean."

"And I was so looking forward to discussing Voltaire tonight." Michael didn't turn from the bathroom mirror.

"I haven't even read Voltaire, asshole."

"You read *Candide*, didn't you?" Michael is always giving you too much credit.

"Nope. Missed that day at paramedic school."

"Well, you can both kill me with one arm tied behind your backs, so we'll call it even."

Pat and Michael bonded over three things: a love of Blue Moon beer served in a glass with a slice of orange, an appreciation of old-school hip-hop, and moderately successful womanizing.

You went out with them, watched, and laughed. You stayed on the sidelines, but it was good to see Michael making up for the time he'd lost in high school. Boys like Michael suffer in towns like Antoine. Halfway through your freshman year you'd made it your mission to protect Michael. But by the time you'd placed your fists on hips and let your cape unfurl, a lot of damage had already been done.

The chatter in the gym subsides when Pat returns to the mat, followed by his new trainer.

"Boys, this is Chris Ahrens, a runner-up at last year's Cross-Fit Nationals."

Chris has dirty blonde hair and skin the color of cappuccino. Her eyes are sparkling blue. Contacts? Jesus. Girls with dark skin and light eyes get whatever they want. And then there's her body. A buck thirty of rip without an ounce of wasted flesh, like the endoskeleton of some larger beast melted down for efficiency. Her smile isn't shy.

"Chris is taking the morning conditioning sessions for the next couple months. Okay?" Pat claps his hands defiantly. "We ready? All right. Have at it, Chris."

Chris walks to the whiteboard. The entire stick stares at her ass—an astoundingly perfect, symmetrical thing of incredible beauty. Chris writes a series of exercises, repetitions, and times on the whiteboard.

"Okay, gents, we know all these, right?" she asks, drawing grunts and a couple "yeahs" from the fighters.

It occurs to you what a hyper-ultra-über male environment Razor is, an utter homosociety. Fighters, trainers, promoters, managers—all dudes.

"Yes. We all know all those exercises, Chris," you say.

"Okay." Chris looks at you with the type of intensity that could bend a spoon. "Give yourselves some room then."

Your knuckleheaded friend Yunior gives you a wink as you and the rest of the boys spread out on the mat.

"We ready?" Chris says. "Okay. Three, two, one—" Then instead of yelling "Go!" as is the CrossFit tradition, she makes all of you jump like punks by whistling between her fingers. Loud. Like someone who's owned large dogs her entire life.

She starts with "burpees." A burpee is a simple thing: jump, then drop to the ground and do a push-up. A simple thing really. But do it twenty times. Follow it with sprints from one end of the mat to the other. Wipe the snot on your forearm. Now do twenty more. Follow it with pull-ups. Now do twenty more. Roll your neck like a fighter. Try to act like it ain't shit. Now do twenty more.

A Tribe Called Quest mash-up—with breakbeats designed to leave jeeps shuddering—thuds through the stereo. But you're in a quiet place. Except for the occasional "yeah" and "you got this," your mind is blank. All you hear is the damp slap of hands and feet on the mat. This is the pleasure of the gym. Bit by bit, that pleasure slow-drips into ache. *Enough.* You want to stop. This is what separates fighters: how far past *enough* can you push? It's more a spiritual question than a physical one. There is no scientific consensus on second winds. Smile at the pain, and it'll fade for a second or two. Now string those seconds together. Michael rolls his eyes when you start talking like this. You don't care. It's the one thing you wish people understood about fighting: the sheer suffering—physical and spiritual—one must endure to become even halfway decent at it.

At the end, you buckle to your knees grinning, then fall onto your back. You're thankful for everything: the mat you're lying on, the very oxygen you're drawing into your lungs. In the aftermath of *enough*, details are sharper, music is crisper, simple cold water is fucking amazing. Everything comes into better focus and it all matters less.

"All right, gents?" Chris is breathing hard but standing ramrod straight. Her tone isn't mocking, but there are a couple levels to her question and everyone on the mat understands. Something about her makes you proud. From your back you give her a thumbs-up and immediately feel self-conscious about it.

You spar with Pat for the rest of the morning. You want to go home to catch a nap before returning that evening, but Pat reminds you about the McKay tape.

In the office, Chris has her feet up on the desk opposite Pat's, while hovering a battery-operated hand fan over her forehead.

"Tape on Simon's next opponent," Pat explains, jutting his chin in your direction.

Chris swings her gunmetal-gray Nikes off the desk. "Mind if I watch?"

"Not at all."

The three of you crowd around Pat's computer. The anticipation of violence transforms the atmosphere in the office into that of a premission TOC.

The first clip opens with shots of a British working-class neighborhood. There's a close-up of an older white guy—you assume a coach—in a hooded sweatshirt and corduroy jacket, pointing at a sign outside a storefront gym that reads "Wolf's Den."

"That's his gym?" you ask Pat.

"I guess."

"Is he the only guy who trains there?"

"I don't think so. Why?"

"Shouldn't it be 'Wolves' Den'? You know: *l, v, e, s,* apostrophe?"

Pat looks at you. Chris laughs.

Pat shakes his head and taps the space bar to restart the clip.

McKay is cartoon-superhero muscular. When he rolls his neck in the prefight clips, his ears brush trapezius muscles. Like you, he's very dark skinned. You find yourself thinking about how, when you were in the sixth grade, kids started calling you "midnight." You thought it sounded cool, like a code name in *GI Joe.* Your mom was not happy when she found out about it.

"What's wrong with 'midnight,' Mom?"

"It's not your name, that's what's wrong with it," Ettie snapped, in a tone that ended the conversation.

On the computer screen, McKay has a heavily tattooed Japanese fighter in the mount. Careers are ended in the mount. That familiar and ferocious schoolyard bully pose—perched on the bottom man's chest, knees under his armpits, carpet-bombing his face with punches. Yep. McKay's a southpaw all right.

"Gonna have to bone up defense on your right side," Pat says.

You nod.

The digital McKay sweeps a heavier opponent and, with the calm of an expert anatomist, shifts through more than a dozen feints until suddenly he's viciously extending his body—forcing his opponent's elbow in the wrong direction.

"A Brit who can roll?" you ask.

A close-up of McKay reveals ears with cartilage that has long since moved past cauliflower into something more akin to stalactites.

"He lived in Rio for a couple years," Pat says apologetically.

And, despite his size, McKay bobs and weaves like a young Ali on his feet—more Gregory Hines than a cave troll.

"I'm blacker than him though," you say, deliberately keeping your eyes on the screen.

Chris breaks the ensuing silence. "Nah. I think he's got you there too."

You wonder what your mom is going to think of Chris.

❀

You start hanging out: coffee after workouts, movies on the weekends. She gets you into "Paleolithic" eating.

"Eat like a caveman?" you repeat.

"Cavemen didn't get cancer."

"Yeah, they got eaten by dinosaurs."

"You do know that the Flintstones were fictitious, right? Prehistoric man didn't actually live at the same time as dinosaurs."

"Says you. I'm an Okie, sweetheart. We believe Jesus rode a dinosaur."

Chris laughs. "Just try it, dumbass."

She has a degree in biology and makes real money on her blog, *Chris's Daily Apple.* You didn't even know it was possible to make money on a blog. You laugh when she tells you that taking a kid to McDonald's is child abuse. Then you understand that she's not joking. Her "subversive" ideas about strength in animals just sound like common sense. If male and female panthers and lions developed their bodies in similar ways, why shouldn't female and male humans? You like that she only named predators. You listen to her voice as she rails on about the epidemic of type 2 diabetes among black Americans and realize the only thing you're that passionate about is yourself.

Chris occupies an odd space in your mind, oscillating between respect—like what you have for Pat—and sexual fantasy. The cliché depresses you. Just another loser whacking off to a chick from his gym.

Two months of training with Chris and you've pummeled your body into a sacrifice to the Fight God. Chris and Pat begin tapering down your workouts, and all that agony starts morphing into power. You're healing into a new—better—100 percent.

🌀

"Are you coming out tonight or going to Chris's?" Michael asks, throwing his messenger bag on the couch next to your feet.

You tepee your book on your chest. "New boss still pissing you off?"

"Huh?" Michael snatches a beer out of the fridge, and his tone slides into that of your high school partner in crime. "Nah. Just, it's Friday night. Pat and I are going out and it would be cool if you came along."

"Not tonight, dude. I'm a wreck."

"It's okay. Two hours of mineral waters could really mess you up for the McKay fight." Michael takes a swig of his beer. "I get it." Some evenings he returns home truly pissy, like New York has talked shit to him all day and by about 18:00 he's started to believe it.

"Since when do you drink from the bottle?" you ask, smiling.

"Whatever." Michael throws you a sparkling water. You catch the bottle and, not thinking, open it immediately. Carbonated water explodes on the couch.

"Shit. Sorry." You rub the damp couch with your hand.

Michael waves it off. "So, seriously, you're going to stay home, masturbate vigorously"—he motions appropriately with a clenched fist—"then watch *Supersize Me* at Chris's place?"

"Something like that."

"What happened to the great Simon Moten? The 'Gangster of Love'?" Michael asks the ceiling. "Okay, I'll tell you what. Bring her out. It seems I'm going to have to get to know this one at some point."

"My, aren't you the magnanimous one this evening."

"That's a mighty big word for you, Balboa."

You laugh. "Fuck you."

"C'mon, give her a call."

At the bar, Chris surprises you by having a mojito. You stick to the sparkling water. You watch Pat and wonder how he can keep this up; it seems inhuman to train the way you guys do and still drink with such purpose. Pat and Michael play the good buddies, talking you up as if you're not present. You get Chris's coat just as Michael and Pat are slipping into sloppy-drunk territory.

Michael gives you a long hug on the sidewalk in front of the bar and then leans into your ear. "I miss you, man."

You kiss Michael on the mouth. Chris cheers. Michael backs off, shocked, laughing.

"Asshole!" He's smiling ear to ear. "You're lucky I'm drunk!"

"You're lucky I'm sober," you respond, winking.

Pat shakes his head. You don't care. This is the closest you've felt to your old self in years.

Chris lives in Hoboken. You walk her to the PATH station at Ninth Street. She asks you to come back to her place. You've been to Chris's apartment before, but something about this invitation feels different. You agree, trying your damndest to appear casually pleased as opposed to breathlessly ecstatic.

Chris makes tea and tells you about her parents, both retired from federal government jobs and living in Maryland. Her family's tight—she sees her parents, brother, and sisters several times a year. Her father's black American. Her mom is German. They met while her father was in the army in Stuttgart. Chris looks at you intently when discussing her "multicultural heritage"—her words. You furrow your brow and nod. You hope that's enough.

You start telling her about Somalia and then stop. You try explaining differently, then stop again. You can't get the words right. It feels like those desperate attempts to continue fucking after going limp. Instead you tell her about growing up with your mom in Oklahoma, about Michael's family, especially Frank. You tell her how the black kids bullied Michael the worst. You tell her about the real glee—the sincere delight—some of them took in calling Michael a "little faggot" while smacking books out of his hands. You tell her that standing up for Michael is one of the few things you've done in your life that you're truly proud of.

"Prouder than you'll feel when you get that belt?" Chris asks.

You open your mouth, then close it.

Chris nudges her fingertips against your knuckles. "You've done a lot to be proud of, Simon."

She's not wearing contacts.

You don't tell her about your son or his mom. One story at a time.

Early the next morning, you emerge from the PATH station on Houston Street. On the sidewalk, rats scurry by post-apocalyptic piles of weekend West Village garbage.

That evening you call Daphne to ask about your son. She doesn't pick up and you don't leave a voice mail.

🌀

At Razor a couple days later, Yunior catches you with a crack like a shotgun slug to the side of the head. You're wearing headgear, but it's easily the cleanest punch you've ever taken in your life. You try to shake it off, but after a minute take a knee.

You squeeze your eyes shut and the darkness shimmers at the edges. You swear you hear the Fight God laughing.

"Shit. Fuck. You okay, Sy?"

"I'm good, Yunior. Just wait 'til I get your ass on the mat next time." You feel like you might throw up.

Pat tells you to go home and not come back until tomorrow. Then he looks at you.

"Don't even think about it," you tell him. "I'm fine."

Chris gets you back to your apartment. You feel a little dizzy on the PATH a couple times, but you're pretty sure you're okay. You imagine what the fighters in your stick are saying now.

"Yeah, he's tough, but he's never *really* been hit."

"Boy's eyes filled up like a Newark storm drain."

"Kanaris could fight, but he isn't a banger like this McKay." Fuck them.

You wave an apoplectic Josephine off the couch and collapse with your head on Chris's lap. Chris dabs an ice pack on your face. Sometime later you wake and open your eyes just enough to see Michael in the kitchen, one hand bracing the doorframe above his head.

"Well, look at this messianic sight," Michael says.

"He's sleeping," Chris whispers.

"Or is he unconscious? You think he can still tell the difference?" Michael's voice is hard, accusatory. "My dad died today."

You sit up and are swept with the feeling of something deeply foul passing from your stomach to your head.

"What? Frank?" you say stupidly. Of course it's Frank. Michael has only one father.

"Heart attack. Your mom tried to call you." Michael points at your mobile on the coffee table. "Your phone's off."

Michael resists your embrace for a moment. Finally, you manage to take him into your arms. Neither of you is in a rush to let go.

Later, the three of you sit facing each other over steaming mugs of chamomile and peppermint. You try to focus but your brain still feels like pancake batter. Michael is saying something about arrangements for the funeral.

"I have a fight, Michael. You know I won't be able to make it."

"You . . . Wait—what?"

"McKay. The fight. I can't leave now."

Michael drops his eyes to the coffee table and exhales hard. You look at Chris, but she won't meet your eyes. Instead she moves to the armrest of Michael's recliner and puts her arm around his shoulders. Michael shrugs her off, and shoots to his feet.

"You know what? Fuck your fight and fuck you."

"Take it easy, Michael."

"No, you fucking take it easy, *bruh*." Michael hasn't imitated your voice in this tone since you were teenagers. It still stings.

"Guys . . ." Chris implores.

"The big hero." Michael snarls at you, and then his voice cracks. "He was your father too. Closest thing you had. But fatherhood doesn't mean shit to you, does it?" He jerks a thumb in Chris's direction. "Did you tell her about Marlon? About Marlon's mother? Did you tell her how a fucking belt is more important than your son?"

Michael pushes you hard in your chest. You barely budge, but not intentionally. If you had expected his shove, you would have let it topple you. If you had expected it, you would have splayed onto your back with abandon. Anything to make Michael hurt a bit less.

"Answer me, motherfucker!"

You raise your hands in surrender.

Michael storms out of the apartment. You let him go.

Chris shows you her palm before you can start explaining, and then she walks out.

It's a relief. You don't want to explain.

Josephine hops onto the recliner and looks at you like she's imagining your brains splattered on the rug.

❁

Night of the fight. You're backstage with Pat. The dressing room is nice—roomy, flat-screen TV, iPod dock, the works.

Pat pulls a cushioned folding chair in front of you. He tears off ten strips of gauze tape and hangs them from the side of the table to your left. You wonder whether he's spoken to Chris or Michael, but not enough to ask. Pat tapes in between your fingers and uses the last two strips to fasten it all in place on each hand. He holds up his palms and you tap them with your fists. Feels good—tight but not too tight.

"Start warming up," Pat tells you.

You jump rope for a minute, stretch, shadowbox, roll your neck, and repeat.

There's a knock at the door. You drop the jump rope to answer it. It's the ref. You recognize him, an older Japanese fellow who presided over two of your early fights—two of the knockouts.

The ref checks the tape on your hands with brisk officiousness, then touches your forearm.

"Be brave," he tells you, a faint smile on his lips.

You don't know how to be anything else. You've whittled yourself into something that cannot splinter, something to which nothing can cleave. You stand immaculate before the clash.

You give the ref a nod. There aren't any more knocks on the door.

9 | The Sacred Disease

From: mathisg8181@hotmail.com
To: tnikuradze@clstmanagement.org
Subject: Re:Re:Re: Are you even writing yet?
Date: August 12, 2008

Hey, Tam.

This is a pretty late draft. Which is my way of saying, I think it's done. First piece since the book on the Panthers. Feels good. Let me know what you think. See you soon!!!!

All my love,
Gabs

Antoine, Oklahoma
September 1992

IT STRUCK MICHAEL first in the Kickapoo convenience store—a jangly electric jolt—like someone flicked the funny bone in his skull.

Simon and I stared as a line of Mountain Dew–tinged saliva dripped from Michael's lips toward the beige Formica table.

Simon's hand shot up to support Michael's sagging chin, and I broke into a nervous laugh, eyes darting between the two older boys.

Simon's expression nosedived, then screeched to a scolding halt. "This ain't a joke, Gabe."

Then, just as suddenly, Michael nodded back into himself, raising his chin from Simon's palm. He reached for a napkin from the metal dispenser on the table, and, blinking damply, swabbed his lips.

Simon flashed us a relieved grin over our red plastic cups of soda. Simon was so dark skinned that when he smiled it was an event, like watching the curtains rise on a play.

I exhaled. As long as Simon wasn't worried, everything would be fine.

That first spasm, the one in the Kickapoo, happened at the beginning of Simon and Michael's freshman year. We spent a lot of time in the Kickapoo that fall. All of us were involved in after-school activities: Simon in football, Michael in French club, and me in sixth-grade jazz dance—a semester-long break from ballet. Our evening walks back to our neighborhood took us by the convenience store–cum–diner–cum–gas station. Most days we ducked in for a slushie and a shit-talking session of *Mortal Kombat II*.

The Kickapoo used to be McCloud 66 and before that the Kwik Stop. Besides the name, the place remained in stasis. Same hot dogs on greasy rotisseries, same advertisements for Milwaukee's Best plastered on the windows, same overhead PA system locked on K-Billy's *Super Sounds of the '70s*, and same parking lot packed on Friday evenings with the posse— upperclassmen spiced with a few who'd already graduated or dropped out—catcalling girls and searching for parties.

Michael called the Kickapoo "a microcosm of everything we hate about this town."

In reply, Simon would cast his gaze to the heavens. "Bitter much?" But we could tell he liked the implied complicity.

Like scrawny high-yellow specters, Michael and I wove invisibly through the Kickapoo parking lot on Friday evenings. While Simon—a three-sport star bumped all the way from freshman to varsity football at the beginning of the school year—fielded calls of "Midnight!" and "'Sup, young buck!" The only hint of athleticism in our household was my competitive dancing, a hobby (along with our shared passion for Dungeons & Dragons and the Marvel Universe) best kept unadvertised.

Interacting with the posse required PhD-level game, and Michael and I didn't even have our undergrad work done. We gave dap hesitantly; we wondered (but never asked) how much malt liquor etiquette demanded be tipped to the pavement; and, while we appreciated a big ass (at least I know I did), we had no idea how much enthusiasm to display for one.

The posse pimped like they were dragging balls and chains on their legs, straining at their crotches as if hefting organs of indescribable weight, and letting entire sentences ooze out the sides of their mouths in two or three mumbled syllables. Their monikers reflected exaggerated exploits and attributes: Dino, Baby Joe, Skinny Pimp, Bushwick, Treetop. Small-town brown boys compensating for their lack of inner-city street cred by overemulating BET's *Rap City.*

And TJ—Thomas James Boyd, All-State linebacker—was their gold-toothed, stoop-jeaned, crisp-Starter-T-shirted king. Like some horrible genetic testament to how slave masters had bred their stock, TJ had made All-State at the most physical position on the football field without even seeming to try all that hard, and took every opportunity to advertise how little he cared about the accomplishment.

"Hey, Midnight," TJ shouted at Simon one Friday evening in the fall of '92. "What you hang with them little faggot Mathis niggers for?" TJ didn't pronounce *nigger* the way he would with his boys, transforming the *er* into an *a*. He said the word like a redneck, with all its venom.

Simon sniffed, thumbing his nose like a prizefighter. "Ask me again and we might have to figure it out."

Simon had been telling us that, since getting bumped to varsity (and thus beating out a posse member for a starting wide receiver spot), his status on the street had shifted. Now TJ was publicly ascertaining just how much. Power's like that—when it shifts, everybody feels it at once.

TJ flicked his tongue over a gold-capped incisor and hawked up a wad of phlegm. He spit, not in our direction exactly, but not too far away from us either.

The posse stubbed out Newports on the heels of their Timbs.

Simon, full of lion-cub swagger, didn't lower his gaze.

Michael and I followed Simon's lead and held our heads up too. Everything we knew about animal kingdom masculinity we learned from watching Simon.

TJ flicked away his cigarette, sending a shower of sparks to the gravel. Then he started toward us—abruptly, violently. I ignored the anxiety clawing at my heart and didn't budge.

With everyone focused on TJ and Simon, only I noticed when—for just half a moment—Michael's eyeballs rolled to milk-glass and his chin tapped his chest. The second time I'd seen the Sacred Disease strike my brother, a week or so after the first.

Then, right on cue, an Antoine Police Department cruiser pulled into the parking lot with lights on but no sirens.

TJ stopped short, close enough that his Brut cologne singed my nostrils. Then he gave Simon dap—the chest-banging kind, as much challenge as greeting—as if that had been his intention from the start. During our weekend workout sessions, Frank had told us how these fist-pounding "five on the black-hand side" handshakes originated with his generation of GIs in Vietnam. Intricate and exhausting spectacles that, even in my exclusion, I found vaguely embarrassing.

The cruiser's tinted window lowered, revealing Officer Bob Novak, ginger hair cut in a fresh high and tight that exposed the near preternaturally pink sides of his head. Novak placed his elbow on the ledge of the cruiser's window, brandishing the Antoine Police Department patch on the starched crease of his short-sleeved gray uniform.

"You boys all right?" Novak spoke to Michael and me, but TJ's and Simon's faces reflected in his aviator sunglasses. "Need a ride home?"

Michael and I answered in unison, "No thank you, sir."

The officer's thin lips pressed into a perfect line. Novak saw exactly how relieved we were to see him and knew enough not to let the posse in on it.

Finally, he spoke. "Okay. Get on home then and tell your father I said hello."

"Yes, sir."

The cruiser was hardly out of the parking lot before the posse broke into drawn-out "dayaaaaams" and "sheeeeeeeets."

Simon laughed with them, but his head remained cocked to one side—a tilt it never lost.

TJ turned to his crew. "I told y'all. Midnight's next."

TJ didn't give up his crown that day. But there had been a concession, and everyone in that parking lot knew it. That was Simon's first taste of something. What exactly—power, leadership, responsibility—I wasn't sure. But I could tell he was hooked.

Novak called Frank first thing the following morning—a Saturday.

Frank had just become the first black deputy warden at Antoine State Prison. Almost a quarter of Antoine's population (ten thousand, according to the sign next to the post office, a number everyone understood didn't include the convicts) was somehow associated with the prison. Our mother was an administrative assistant at the facility. Ms. Ettie worked as a counselor there. Only four COs at Antoine State Prison held the rank of warden. All save one were, like Frank, Vietnam veterans.

When the childless Novaks ran into our family in town, Bob would squeeze Michael's and my shoulders and punctuate every sentence to Frank with "Warden." Meanwhile his wife—beaming through glasses thick enough to blind you if the light hit them right—would exclaim, "I just can't stop reading about these two in the paper. This one with his dance competitions and the other in National Honor Society!"

Afterward, in the back seat of our wood-paneled station wagon, Frank would grumble, "Those Antoine grays are the only uniform half those hick-cops have ever worn."

But I never forgot how Novak looked out for us in the Kickapoo parking lot that day. The tough-guy nod that Frank bestowed on Novak—and none of the other Antoine cops—indicated that my father never forgot it either.

"I want to talk to you boys," Frank announced that Saturday morning.

Simon, Michael, and I were stretched on couches and beanbags in our basement playing Super Nintendo—our regular weekend configuration.

Simon's dad wasn't around. At all. For as far back as it mattered, Frank's "you boys" meant the three of us.

Frank sat on the recliner, elbows resting on his thighs, biceps straining against the sleeves of a T-shirt emblazoned with the First Cavalry Division's bumblebee-colored insignia.

I hit pause, and we all straightened.

Now, as I struggle to remember that particular conversation, the only phrase I can recall is "Don't let your mouth write a check your ass can't cash." A slightly updated version of the speech we'd suffered all our lives: Be strong, but not too strong. Be brave, but not too brave. The speech Michael dubbed "The Injustice Is Inevitable, Conduct Yourselves Accordingly Spiel." The longer renditions described brown boys with craniums cracked while patting their jackets for cigarettes; brown boys, in interrogation rooms reeking of ammonia, inducted into lives that would be more about prison than anything else; brown boys spoken of in the hushed tones reserved for bad news. The world hunted brown boys from all sides, and its best agents were men in uniform and other brown boys. The only difference was the question preceding the violence. The men in uniform wanted to know where you were going. The other brown boys wanted to know where you were from. Being in a position to be asked either question meant you were already wrong. Frank addressed the three of us that day, but we all knew he was mostly speaking to Simon. He feared for Simon most. We all did. The world hunts all brown boys, but none more ruthlessly than the very brave— these the world made examples of.

"All right." Frank rolled his neck and massaged his shoulder between his thumb and pointer finger. He would supervise a shift at the prison that evening. "I'm going back to bed."

✹

Michael's spasms came and went. Months passed and he'd be fine. Then I'd find my older brother shivering on the couch in our basement with *The Once and Future King* drool splattered on his face. The adolescent precept of releasing information to adults on a strictly need-to-know basis kept us from telling any of our parents—not even Frank, whom all of us were close to—about the episodes. But it wasn't like we went out of the way to hide it from them; looking back, it seems almost as if the disease cloaked itself from the adults in our lives.

By the spring of '95, it was Simon calling the shots in the Kickapoo parking lot. TJ spent two unsuccessful years playing football at a junior college in Kansas and, after flunking out, returned to his mother's place in Antoine. TJ told everyone he would be enlisting in the Marine Corps in the fall. Meanwhile he could be found at the Kickapoo most evenings, hanging around the parking lot and mattering much less. The Kickapoo was the court of King Simon now, first of his name.

One evening that spring, near the end of Michael and Simon's junior year—when school had whittled down to year-book signings and beer-fueled evenings at the lake—the three of us looked up from an after-school snack of chili dogs and Sunkist sodas to a group of out-of-town girls entering the Kickapoo.

"Ahhhhh, yeah." Simon twisted around in his chair. "Around the way girls."

We steeled ourselves for Simon's transformation from our comic-book-quoting buddy to Oklahoma's spine and marrow: the small-town football star.

One of the girls—with Afro puffs and curves beyond her years—made eye contact with me. Her almond-eyed stare while passing our table was three-fourths flirtation and a quarter challenge.

I stirred the ice in my soda with a straw.

The girls settled into a booth at the opposite end of the convenience store.

Simon winked at me. "Soul meets soul when eyes meet eyes. Does your true love stand recognized?" A line from *Elfquest*, one of our favorite comics; the sort of reference Simon loved but wouldn't have dreamed of making with the platoon of simpletons he now led at school.

"Do you know her?" Michael asked.

"No," I whispered. "Do you guys?"

"Nope, but we ought to get to know them." Simon, basking in his heartland herodom, snuck his head around me and arched an eyebrow in the girls' direction. "And enough with all this chickenshit whispering."

"Will you please stop looking at them," I pleaded.

Then Michael nodded out, face slouching toward the chili dog on his plastic blue plate. Simon braced my brother. A short one. Less than thirty seconds.

"What're they like, Michael?" I asked. "The fits, I mean."

Simon, who'd been raising his hand to make some pronouncement, settled down to listen. Of course, we'd discussed the convulsions before, but mostly in terms of damage control. How not mentioning the spasms to our parents kept Michael out of some kind of counseling or special education arrangement that would have only made things harder on him (and all of us, really) at school. Or what triggered the fits (which, as near as we could tell, was stress or absolutely nothing). But we'd never really talked about what the fits actually felt like. Under Simon's intense gaze—determined to lead me to the holy grail of a girlfriend whether I liked it or not—I figured now was as good a time as any to delve deeper.

"You know, the weird thing is the moment before it happens it's awesome." Michael rubbed his chin with the back of his hand. "Literally awesome. I have this . . . this amazing flash of clarity. It's hard to describe."

Many years later, while researching an article comparing Dostoyevsky to Eminem—my first successful pitch to a big magazine—I learned of the left temporal lobe seizures the Russian novelist suffered. Before the onset of a fit, Dostoyevsky described a moment of ecstatic satori "worth ten years of regular life." A condition neurologists still refer to as "Dostoyevsky's Epilepsy." What the ancient Greeks called "The Sacred Disease." But at thirteen years old in the Kickapoo convenience store I knew none of this. Otherwise I certainly would have brought it up to fend off what Simon said next.

"You should ask her to dance."

"Ask her to dance," I repeated in the brutish tone Michael and I usually reserved for imitating Simon's conversations with the posse; he hated when we spoke to him like that. "We are in the Kickapoo, for chrissake."

Simon continued, undeterred, "Yeah, man, ask her to dance. No matter what else happens in her life you will always be that dude who asked her to dance in the Kickapoo. That one *ballsy* dude who asked her to dance in a fucking gas station." Then he leaned across the table and spoke slowly, like he expected me to take notes. "In my experience, if you have a chance at a boss-player move, it's best to give it a try. It ain't gonna hurt you."

Michael shrugged. "The Gangster of Love actually has a point for once."

I turned from Michael to Simon and back again. I have to hand it to those two—their expressions didn't budge.

I nodded and stood. My gait as I walked toward the girls' table was not, I feared, that of someone making "a boss-player move." But rather that of a boy facing two of his greatest fears: pretty girls and starting conversations.

K-Billy's *Super Sounds of the '70s* was playing on the overhead audio (the same system over which Kickapoo clerks would announce Skittles were on sale). And that's how Jagger's homage to the devil congealed into an anecdote that three small-town brown boys never tired of repeating.

"Would you like to dance?"

"Dance?" Her friends laughed. "Here?" She swept her arm to indicate the hot-dog rotisserie under the bubble-glass sneeze guard, a mom with three kids slurping on fountain drinks in a nearby booth, the skateboarders on the *Streetfighter Alpha II* video game in the corner.

Flushed with newfound confidence, I held out my hand. "C'mon."

I had forgotten something that Simon had not: I could dance and had been doing so competitively for more than four years by then. The moment before she took my hand, I glanced back and watched the curtains rise on Simon's smile.

That evening in the Kickapoo, the clerks, the manager, the mom and her kids, the guys on the video game—everyone stopped what they were doing to watch me lead my first girlfriend, Jennifer, on a tiptoed waltz between the convenience store's laminated tables.

I met Jennifer's stare in a spin to avoid a mop bucket and everyone laughed. When the song ended, I bowed and held my new girlfriend's hand as if she were a countess. The Kickapoo burst into applause. And there was Simon—who'd led me to the promised land—standing in the plastic booth, clapping, and laughing with his entire body.

Then, not five minutes later in the Kickapoo parking lot, Simon sniggered with the rest of the posse at TJ's play-by-play of his latest sexual conquest.

"Good old Sally Anne," TJ proclaimed. "Dirty blonde, small tits, not much of an ass."

With his enlistment in the marines impending, TJ's sole mission in life seemed to be to nail everything with breasts and a pulse before shipping out.

Simon pursed his lips. "When you say 'dirty blonde,' you're talking about the hair on her head, right?"

Simon laughed just hard enough along with TJ and the rest.

Later, when it was just the three of us, Michael asked Simon, "Why do you play the buffoon with them?"

Simon shrugged. "Fuck's sake, Michael. We're just bullshitting."

PhD-level game made boys like Simon—boys with good hearts—sound like monsters. But even I understood that, for most of these boys old enough to mistake themselves for men, these misguided expressions of masculinity *were* jokes. But not for TJ. His boasts were different, veering away from simple crass descriptions into the type of talk that elicited laughter of the lynch-mob variety.

TJ's vivid reenactment of the girl's impassioned cries, alternating stress between words ("*Oh*, Thomas! Oh, *Thomas!*") rendered whatever actually happened between the bastard and Sally irrelevant.

An air of county fairs and church socials hung around a girl like Sally, and she had the boyfriend to go with it. Zack Stanton, a farm-strong offensive lineman from the neighboring town of McCloud. Simon knew Zack, described him as one of those bred-tough country white boys who, on the football field, treated their bodies like rental cars. When we ran into Zack's type in Simon's presence, we sensed the razor's edge of respect and tension between them. The respect and tension of boys who'd spilt sweat together at football camps and tasted victory and defeat on opposing sides of the same fields since junior high.

In places like McCloud and Antoine, teenagers schedule fights like high school dances. TJ and Zack's was slated for that Friday in the Kickapoo parking lot. By the end of the week, old slights and grudges between Zack's crowd and the posse had upped the ante to a group brawl.

But in the lead-up, everyone at school focused on Simon. Leadership resides where people think it resides, and Simon had absolutely no intention of recusing himself from the responsibilities it carried. In fact, Simon canvassed like a politician in the lunchroom that week. "I know all of y'all gonna be there Friday to back up one of our own, right?"

Since he was an athlete, people assumed Simon could scrap. But Michael and I knew that, not counting wrestling matches, he hadn't actually been in a fight since grade school. This would not be a wrestling match. Zack outweighed Simon by a good seventy pounds, and the offensive lineman looked like he could punch his weight.

On Friday evening, I found Simon and Michael huddled in our basement.

"I'm coming."

Simon shook his head. "You're too young for this shit."

I crossed my arms, stood still, held his gaze.

Simon took in my spot-on approximation of his patented head tilt.

"Okay." Simon paused, turned to Michael, then back to me. "Okay," he repeated.

The three of us trudged to the Kickapoo under the streetlights' amber glow, a million crickets chirping the song of the Oklahoma dusk.

"Scared?" Simon asked.

The older boys waited for me to speak. But certain that my words would waver, I held my tongue.

"Yeah, Simon. I'm fucking scared." Michael hardly ever cursed.

"Me too," Simon said gently, then, with a team-captainesque tone that fell flat, he added, "Get your minds right."

"Remind me," Michael said, "because I keep forgetting. Why exactly are we defending a bully who talks like a rapist?"

"No." Simon pounded his chest. "I'm defending all of us."

I wondered if Simon truly believed that. He might have. He certainly never stopped searching for demons to slay.

A cloud of savagery choked the air in the Kickapoo parking lot. Blunts and bottles of Old E passed from hand to hand while the latest Tupac joint bumped sonic confidence from the speakers of open car doors.

Back in elementary, I thrived on misery.
Left me alone, I grew up amongst a dying breed.

For the first time, TJ welcomed Michael and me into the sea of scowls, fist bangs, and shoulder-to-chest hugs.

"My niggas!"

It stung worse without the *er* on the end; now it reduced us to nothing but one of them. *You're here. You're just like us.*

"Y'all ready to show these motherfuckers some Antoine hospitality!" TJ shouted.

Michael leaned into me and Simon and whispered, "A celebration of ignorance."

Simon looked past Michael to TJ. "Lemme get a square."

"Shit, I'll do you one better than that." TJ tapped the back of a box of Swisher Sweets, then held his Bic under the cigar as Simon took a few leisurely puffs, no one looking in their direction but everyone watching.

Zack's crew arrived by the pickup load. Viking-wild good old boys with belt buckles the size of bricks, spitting tobacco through their teeth. Cans of Pabst Blue Ribbon clanked out of the bed of their trucks onto the parking lot as White Zombie's testosterone-laced guitar riffs competed with Tupac's thumping bravado.

The posse jostled Michael and me—lips, fists, and asshole cinched—to the rear of the crowd. Simon stood at the front of the pack, where Zack and TJ were roaring the fucking hows and fucking whys of the fucking beatdown they would give the fucking other. What their cursing lacked in creativity it made up in spit and fire.

One of Zack's crew broke from the crowd and coldcocked Simon with a bottle of Coors.

"It's the punches you don't see coming," Frank used to say, "that'll knock you out."

The crash crescendoed into a din of shouts and fists as the world splintered into dozens of individual battles.

My heart staccatoed in my chest as a target—a wispy, blond mustache under a frayed maroon ball cap—came into view. I swung twice, missed completely, and lost my footing.

As I lay supine on the gravel, someone planted a shitkicker in my ribs. Damp clumps burned through my throat and filled my mouth. Sparks danced on the edges of my vision. I lost the direction of safety and coiled into the fetal position, gobbled up by the madness.

My eyes snapped open for Michael. I found him, head bobbing to a tune only he could hear, slumped against the hood of a Ford Escort, a forgotten cog in a machine of mass destruction.

I thrust myself onto all fours and stumble-lunged toward my brother. Enveloped in chaos, I gripped Michael's shoulders and searched for an escape.

Sirens, screeching tires, and authoritative shouts surfaced in the anarchy. Both sides bolted like phantoms.

Simon jackknifed out of the haze of darting figures, wrested Michael down behind the Ford, and pressed him upright against the side of the vehicle. We huddled behind the car, watching my older brother's head loll aimlessly between his shoulders.

Crack! Crack! Crack! Crack! Crack!

The shattering peal of gunshots reverberated through my guts, snatching at the inside of my throat. Michael jerked back into consciousness.

We cowered behind the engine block while VHF handhelds squawked and boots crunched gravel. Three brown boys. In fear for their lives.

"Raise your hands." Pebbles, blood, and an eerie calm were plastered to Simon's dark face. "Slowly, okay?"

Michael and I exposed our palms and rose with Simon to our feet.

Two terrifyingly Caucasian Antoine cops approached, Beretta barrels pegged to our chests, expressions leaving no doubt as to our disposability.

I don't think any of us heard TJ's voice during the melee—I know I hadn't—but we all saw his face afterward. Under the streetlights' dull glow, I exchanged a long look with TJ's wide-eyed corpse.

Simon went on to see the faces of many dead in his lifetime. Dusty faces in a village in Helmand Province—old, young, male, female—all frozen in the same astonished expression.

The gaunt, emaciated faces at Banadir Hospital in Mogadishu. The face of his friend Wes—shit and guts spilling from his abdomen—as he withered into a corpse, like a piece of wax paper caught in a flame.

"But only TJ's face returns to me in dreams," Simon said.

TJ's face was his face. Michael's face. My face. The face of a brown boy snarling at the world. A brown boy with crimson-tinged, eight-ball hemorrhaged eyes, sprawled on the gravel like roadkill. A brown boy who could have been any of us before we became men.

According to the *Antoine Herald*, twenty-year-old Thomas James Boyd died of multiple gunshot wounds to the chest while resisting arrest. The question of whether TJ was reaching into his pocket when Novak told him to raise his hands was never answered well. The question of whether TJ was armed was; the only things in TJ's pockets were his wallet and a pack of cheap honey-tipped cigars.

Novak stopped his colleagues from handcuffing us in the Kickapoo parking lot.

"I'll . . . I'll call your father."

I got a good look at Novak when he said it. I searched his features for malice, glee, condescension—anything that would help me hate him—but found nothing.

Novak supported Simon to the ambulance and sat the three of us in the back of the rig. Then he slammed the ambulance doors shut and tapped the rear-facing window with his knuckles.

Michael and I sat on a bench in the back of the vehicle watching a paramedic press bandages against Simon's face and intermittently suction his airway with a thin plastic tube. My sore ribs were hardly worth mentioning next to Simon—grimy with beer, dried blood, and the bright red fresh stuff from a gash in his cheek. Michael—fresh faced and somehow serene—noticed that I noticed when he placed his hand on top of Simon's and squeezed. The Sacred Disease had hauled my brother through the demon's lair without a smudge.

Frank rushed to the hospital with Ettie.

Under examining-room lights, the four of us watched as a nurse held a finger under Simon's chin and surveyed the damage.

"That's going to need stitches," the nurse said to the adults, then to Simon, "Hold that bandage in place."

She clanked materials for the suture onto a steel tray.

"Where's the other boy?" Frank asked.

The nurse didn't look up from the curved surgical needle she was threading. "Which one?"

Frank's glare scorched from me to Michael, then finally seared into Simon.

"Zack." Simon pressed the bandage to the side of his face as he spoke. "Zack Stanton."

"They're prepping him for surgery. Internal bleeding."

Zack Stanton walked with a limp for the rest of his life.

"Idiots." The three of us winced every time Frank spoke. "Talented. Gifted. Y'all think those words make you exempt?" Froth formed at the edge of my father's mouth. "The only difference between you three and that kid in the morgue is timing."

"Frank." Ettie, dark and regal as ever, placed her hand on my father's forearm. "Give me a second with them."

The years have mixed the memory of Ms. Ettie's more militant version of the "injustice is inevitable" spiel. What I remember most from the hospital was the glimpse I caught as Frank barged through the swinging examining-room doors.

Novak stood in the hallway with two of his colleagues, their faces cemented with unmistakable pride. Real cops.

Novak lawyered up but needn't have bothered. No one wanted to press charges: not our parents, not Ettie, not Zack's folks, not even TJ's mother. Novak worked a desk job for a couple months. He was back on patrol by the end of Simon and Michael's senior year.

❀

I was twenty-five and teaching English in Ukraine when my mother called with news of Frank's death from a heart attack. Simon and Michael were twenty-eight, both in New York. Simon training for a fight. Michael working for the same fashion magazine he'd been with since graduating from Columbia.

"Simon's not coming to the funeral," Michael told me over a line from the East Coast.

"Yeah," I replied cautiously. "He told me."

"Ain't that a motherfucker?" Michael cursed more now.

We buried Frank in Antoine, on a Tuesday in October.

I didn't notice TJ's plot as we carried Frank's flag-draped coffin past the burnt-orange oak trees. But Michael pointed it out as we silently filed out of the cemetery.

THOMAS JAMES BOYD
DECEMBER 12, 1975–APRIL 14, 1995
BROTHER. SON. FRIEND.

Ettie drove our mother home. We stopped at the Kickapoo—now Stax!Stax!Stax!—on the way back to the house. I had a chili dog, Michael a sparkling water.

"Simon's favorite drink now," Michael said, holding up the plastic green bottle of Perrier. "His demon-slayer diet. I don't think he's had a beer since he started fighting."

I willed Michael to stop speaking. It didn't work.

"You know, I never had another fit after leaving this place." He glanced around the convenience store as if it had been personally responsible for the spasms. Then, looking out the storefront window, Michael smiled, and I was glad he wasn't smiling at me. "Maybe I was just allergic to Oklahoma."

"Maybe."

Michael capped and uncapped his bottle, continued staring out the window. "We got lucky here. That night in the parking lot."

I watched the lie distort my older brother's face.

Each of Michael's seizures had been ordained, the one that shielded us that night anointed as the last. The Sacred Disease had run its course, leaving us as strong and brave as we dared.

Dewaine Farria's writing has appeared in the *New York Times*, the *Rumpus*, *War on the Rocks*, *CRAFT*, and the *Southern Humanities Review*. He coedits the *Maine Review*'s weekly "Embody" Column. He holds an MFA in creative writing from the Vermont College of Fine Arts and an MA in international and area studies from the University of Oklahoma, where—as a David L. Boren National Security Education Program Fellow—he studied at the Kyiv Linguistic Institute. As a US Marine, he served in Jordan and Ukraine. Besides his stint in the military, he spent most of his professional life working for the United Nations Department of Safety and Security (UNDSS), with assignments in the North Caucasus, Kenya, Somalia, and Occupied Palestine. He was awarded UNDSS's Bravery Award for his actions during an attack on the United Nations Development Programme compound in Mogadishu in June 2013. He lives in Manila with his wife, three children, two cats, and a dog. This is his first novel.